WILD TIDE

TYSON WILD BOOK FOUR

TRIPP ELLIS

WELCOME

Want more books like this?

You'll probably never hear about my new releases unless you join my newsletter.

SIGN UP HERE

1

"I'm sorry, am I interrupting your beauty sleep?" Sheriff Wayne Daniels barked into the phone. His harsh voice blasted through the tiny speaker as I held it to my ear.

"Yeah, kind of," I said with a healthy dose of sarcasm, wiping the sleep from my eyes.

"It's not helping. You're still ugly," Daniels quipped. Where's that numb-nuts friend of yours?"

"He's in Miami."

"What's he doing there?"

"I don't know," I stammered, knowing full well what JD was doing there.

"I tried calling him but he won't pick up. What the hell am I paying you two for? You're never around?"

"You're not paying us, remember? We're volunteers," I grumbled.

"Well, get your volunteer ass out of bed and meet me on the

dock in five minutes. I'm picking you up. We've got another body."

Sheriff Daniels hung up the phone without supplying any further details. I'd been back in Coconut Key less than a week and there was already trouble on the horizon.

I crawled out of bed, pulled on a pair of shorts and slipped on a T-shirt. I grabbed my Kydex holster and press-checked my weapon, then slipped the holster in my waistband for an appendix carry. I put on a pair of sneakers and grabbed my shiny gold Deputy Sheriff's badge.

There was no time for breakfast, but I grabbed a Diet Coke from the fridge as I passed through the galley.

While we were in Monaco, Jack had contracted a serious, incurable case of yacht envy. The 70 foot, *Valkyrie Sportfish* he bought was the most notable symptom.

I wasn't complaining.

He had named it *Wild Tide* in honor of yours truly. It was my new home, and I was still getting used to the accommodations. It was damn near twice the size of Jack's old boat.

She had two upgraded MTU 16V 2000 series engines, was tournament rigged, and had just about every factory option. The large cockpit had a teak deck, centerline bait well, tuna door, a fighting chair, and a below deck gyro-stabilizer. To port, there was a built-in fish box in the deck, and to starboard, a live bait well. Forward of the cockpit was a mezzanine with a built-in refrigerator and freezer, as well as a lounge and a retractable sunshade. Centerline of the mezzanine, a hatch led below to the main engine room. The engines were immaculate, painted in *Awlgrip* white, making a top speed of 43 knots.

The boat had sleek, aggressive lines. The hull was painted in navy, with a white superstructure. She had an upgraded Lewmar bow anchor with 350 feet of anchor chain.

The salon was nothing short of luxurious. Upon entry, there was an L-shaped setee to starboard, with storage below. To port, a staircase led up to the flybridge. There was a day head positioned near the main entrance to the salon. A high/low flatscreen TV provided entertainment for the salon with satellite capability.

Forward of the main salon was the galley, complete with microwave, ice maker, refrigerator, and freezer. There was a dual sink, glass stovetop, microwave, dishwasher, and trash compactor. Opposite the galley, to starboard, was a dining area with high/low table.

Just aft of the galley, to port, was a bar with an ice maker and stem storage. Forward of the galley was a storage area that housed the A/V systems. The starboard stairs led down to four cabins, including a crew cabin with stacked bunks that had direct access to the engine room.

A few steps down the companionway was the master suite, to port. It had a queen berth, en suite with stall shower, large flatscreen display, and luxurious cherry-wood panelling.

Adjacent to the master was a full size stackable washer and dryer. Another compartment of stackable bunks offered modest accommodations for guests, and a VIP stateroom at the bow with a queen berth and en suite provided a more luxurious stay.

The flybridge was essentially a smaller, second salon. There was an L-shaped settee to starboard, and to port, a minibar with refrigerator and ice maker. Forward of the compartment was the state-of-the-art helm with seating for five. Multiple displays provided a variety of options and information. There were controls for underwater lighting, a VHF radio, engine monitors, throttle control, bow and stern thruster joysticks, gyro controls, shipboard monitoring, FLIR, and night vision. There were depth meters, SONAR, GPS navigation, and a host of other controls. Aft of the flybridge was a skydeck with helm controls, and a small settee.

I didn't ask how much JD paid for the boat, and I didn't want to know.

I moved through the salon and stepped into the cockpit and breathed in the fresh salty air of the morning. Gulls squawked overhead, and the amber rays of morning sun hit my face, warming my skin.

I paused for a moment to enjoy the brief calmness before the chaos.

I met Sheriff Daniels as he pulled to the end of the dock in his patrol boat. I climbed on board and said good morning to Brenda—the medical examiner, Bill—a crime scene photographer, and Roger—a forensics guy.

Daniels throttled up and piloted the boat out of the harbor, then brought the boat *on plane*. We skated across the sea, smacking the waves, and a fine mist of saltwater sprayed my face with each undulation.

I didn't bother asking what was going on. I'd find out soon

enough. Besides, Sheriff Daniels probably didn't know any more details than I did.

Unfortunately, another body turning up in Coconut Key was nothing unusual. The island paradise certainly had a dark side.

2

The mangled body lay on the deck of a fishing trawler, twisted in a net. The skin was pale and ghostly, and the carcass looked like it had an encounter with a propeller or two.

Large chunks of flesh were missing, and the edges were frayed—the body had provided a few tasty morsels for numerous sea creatures.

A few fish flopped on the deck beside the body, gasping for air, but the victim had long since drawn his last breath. The man's face was bloated, and his opened eyes were milky orbs that stared into nothing, like a zombie's eyes. He had dark ratty hair, twisted and frazzled from the sea. He wore shorts, a T-shirt, and deck shoes.

The smell emanating from the body was enough to curl your nose hairs. That, mixed with the fishy odor of the boat, made me glad I had skipped breakfast.

Gulls squawked overhead, hovering on the breeze. They

swooped down to the deck, trying to peck a few morsels from the remains.

A deckhand kept shooing them away.

Brenda went to work immediately, examining the body. Flashes from the crime scene photographer lit up the area.

The fishing boat rocked back and forth with the waves. Roger and Bill did their best to steady themselves, but they didn't look too fond of being on the water. Roger's skin tone wasn't that far off from the victim's, and he looked like he was going to grab the gunwale at any moment and make a contribution to the sea.

"When did you find the body?" Sheriff Daniels asked.

"Maybe half an hour ago," the skipper said. "We called you right away."

The skipper had dark hair, a weathered face, and a chin made of steel. A few days of stubble peppered his face, and his crooked smiled revealed more than a few missing teeth. His skin was dark and leathery from years in the sun. This was a man who worked his knuckles to the bone.

"Has anyone touched the body?" Daniels asked.

"We pulled him on board, set him on the deck, then called you," the skipper said. "There may have been some incidental contact. But where he lay is where he lay."

"Where did you find him?" Daniels asked.

"Right here," the skipper said. "We dropped anchor, and I noted the GPS coordinates."

Sheriff Daniels asked Brenda, "Any idea how long the body has been in the water?"

"I'm just guessing, but this level of decomposition looks like three or four days. I'll know more when I get the remains back to the lab."

"Any ID?" Daniels asked.

"Brenda shook her head. "No wallet. Nothing. But Sheriff... I think this is Glenn Parker."

The sheriff tilted his head to the side like a curious dog and surveyed the remains. "I'll be damned. I think you're right."

"Did any of you know this man?" Sheriff Daniels asked the crew.

They all shook their heads.

"I've pulled a lot of things out of the water over the years, but never something like this," the skipper said.

Sheriff Daniels took down the crew's names and contact information. After the investigators were done, we loaded the remains onto the Sheriff's patrol boat and headed back to shore.

"What do you think, boss? Guy falls overboard, drowns, gets carved up by a passing boat?" I postulated, hoping it would be that simple.

"If that *is* Glenn Parker, he was an experienced yachtsman. I think it would be unlikely he fell overboard and drowned. But stranger things have happened," Daniels said with a shrug.

At the station, we transferred the body to the dock and set it atop a gurney, and I helped Brenda move the remains into the ME's van. Her office had recently moved to a more spacious facility with additional room for records storage. A separate laboratory building provided storage of the bodies, autopsy rooms, and testing facilities.

"When is tweedle-dum getting back from Miami?" the sheriff asked.

I shrugged.

"The mayor's charity gala is coming up and I want you two there. I want Coconut Key's finest in attendance." His face crinkled with disapproval. "Well, maybe not Coconut Key's *finest*, but perhaps you two can fake it for an evening?"

I flashed a light-hearted scowl. "Can you give me a lift back to *Diver Down?*"

He looked at me like that was the craziest thing he'd ever heard. "What do I look like, a taxicab? I've got work to do."

"Did you switch to decaf?" I asked, noting his grumpiness.

His eyes narrowed at me.

I flashed a bright smile to contrast his stern gaze. "Okay. I'll catch you later."

I caught a cab back to *Diver Down* and took a seat at the bar.

Madison was behind the counter, but she wasn't doing a very good job. A guy at the end of the bar had her completely enthralled. She hung on his every word and giggled at any attempt at humor he made. After a few minutes, I cleared my throat, trying to get her attention.

Harlan leaned in and muttered in my ear. "Give it up. None

of us exist. She hasn't taken her eyes off the pretty boy in the last 20 minutes. Been like this for the last few weeks. If the service gets much worse, I'm going over to *Pirates' Cove*."

Harlan was a regular. He had white hair, a slightly crooked nose that ended in a point, and a generally grumpy disposition.

"Maddie," I shouted across the bar.

She finally looked my way.

I waved her over, and she excused herself from the pretty boy and sauntered my way.

"Harlan needs another beer, and I'd like to get something to eat."

Madison grabbed a longneck from a tub of ice and popped the top with an opener she slung from the back pocket of her jean shorts. She spun the opener like a gunslinger from the Wild West and slid the amber bottle across the counter to Harlan.

"I'll take a turkey club sandwich, and a Diet Coke," I said.

"Anything else?" she asked, flatly.

"Who is your new friend?"

"His name is Ryan, and I happen to like him, so be nice."

I smiled. "What? I'm always nice."

She gave me an incredulous look.

"Is he your new boyfriend?"

"Yes, as a matter of fact, he is," she said with pride, turning her nose up.

"Don't you think you should introduce us?"

"You're not my father. You don't get approval over my dating life."

"Newsflash," I said. "I don't care who you date. I'm just mildly curious. I went away for a few weeks, and now you have a new boyfriend."

"It's funny how life happens when you're away." She was full of sass.

"How did you two lovebirds meet?"

Her eyes narrowed at me. She was hesitant to answer. "Online."

"Online? I didn't realize you were that desperate."

She scowled at me. "I'm not desperate. It's how people meet these days. I'm a busy, successful woman, and I don't have time for socializing. I'm certainly not going to date customers, and since I have no real social life, that leaves me with few options. Not that I have to explain myself to you."

There was a moment of tense silence before she continued, "And you, of all people, are the last one to give me dating advice. When was the last time you had a real relationship?"

"I have real relationships all the time," I protested.

"One that lasted more than 15 minutes?"

I feigned indignation. "I have plenty of relationships that last longer than 15 minutes, thank you very much. I'm no two pump chump."

Madison rolled her eyes. "TMI. If you'll excuse me, I have other customers."

Harlan chuckled, then muttered, "As if they matter."

Madison shot him a look.

"I just call 'em like I see 'em, and since you've been dating that fella, service in here's gone down the shitter."

Madison took a deep breath. "I apologize, Harlan, if I've been distracted lately."

She smiled and batted her eyelashes at him. She jiggled a little, and her bikini top drew Harlan's attention.

"I reckon it's okay for a pretty young thing to get distracted by a fella. As long as things get back to normal around here. Like I was telling Tyson, I'd hate to take my business elsewhere."

Madison made a pouty face. "Now Harlan, where would you go? The food at *Pirates' Cove* sucks, and they certainly don't have the hospitality."

Madison leaned against the bar, pushing her cleavage together.

Harlan's eyes bulged at the sight. "I guess you're right about that." He swallowed hard. "*Pirates' Cove* doesn't have near the hospitality," he said, talking into her bikini top.

Madison chuckled and pushed away from the bar. She knew how to keep the regulars around.

She spun around and almost skipped down the counter to Ryan. She whispered something in his ear and he climbed off the bar stool and strolled my way. He extended his hand,

and a brilliant smile that belonged in a toothpaste commercial curled on his face as he introduced himself. "Nice to meet you, Tyson. I'm Ryan. I've heard a lot of good things about you."

"Now I know you're lying," I said with a grin.

He had an overly firm, try-hard grip. And there was something phony about him.

I disliked him instantly.

Ryan chuckled. "Seriously, Madison said her older brother always looked out for her and threatened to beat up the guys she dated if they screwed her over."

"Well, that really hasn't changed," I said, modestly, staring him down.

Ryan chuckled nervously again. "Well, I promise, she's in good hands."

"I'll bet," I said, dryly.

There was an awkward pause.

"Well, I've gotta run. It was nice meeting you." He turned his attention to my sister. "Maddy, I'll see you tonight?"

Her eyes sparkled. "Absolutely!"

Ryan excused himself and left.

"He seems like a fine young man," I said trying to be magnanimous.

"He's nice. And I really like him."

I raised my hands innocently. "I'm not going to run him off.

I'm glad you met someone new that makes you happy." I tried to minimize the snarky tone in my voice.

Madison's eyes narrowed at me again. "So, that's it? No snide comments? No dire warnings?"

I shrugged. "You're a grown woman. You can make your own decisions. I mean, you've done a background check on him, haven't you?"

She scoffed. "No! He's a good guy, and I trust my own judgment."

"Okay," I said, surrendering almost too easily.

"Like you run background checks on all the floozies you date?"

"They are not floozies. Not all of them. But, point taken."

Madison stared at me waiting for the other shoe to drop. I think she was expecting me to put up more of an argument. Madison had always been a free spirit, and she was the type to fall fast and hard—often to her detriment. She had some real loser boyfriends in the past, but I was trying to keep an open mind.

Madison attended to the customers she had been neglecting, and the patrons around the bar seemed relieved that the pretty boy had gone. They might actually get served in a timely fashion now.

If she wasn't going to run a background check on Ryan, I sure as hell was.

3

"Tell me good news," I said, answering JD's call.

"Prosecution just offered a plea deal. Two years, deferred adjudication. If Scarlett doesn't screw up while she's on probation, it will be expunged from her record. $3000 fine. No jail time. The lawyer thinks we should take the deal."

"How does Scarlett feel about that?"

"She's mulling it over. If she stays on the straight and narrow, it's like it never happened."

"I'm sure she'll make the right call."

"When has she ever made the right call?"

Jack's daughter hadn't exercised the best judgment as of late.

"Maybe this is the beginning of a new, more responsible, Scarlett?" It was an optimistic thought at best.

A grim chuckle escaped Jack's lips. "Yeah, right." He sighed. "Anything happening back on the island?"

"Just another dead body."

I filled JD in on the details and told him I'd call him as soon as I heard from the medical examiner.

I sat at the bar, shooting the shit with Harlan. He was a former Marine and was at Khe Sanh when the base was under siege. He had countless war stories, but the current battle he faced seemed like one of the toughest yet.

A commercial for the evening news came on the TV behind the bar. A local reporter announced, "A new development has some local residents crying foul!"

The preview cut to an attorney. "We feel that the acquisition of this land is in violation of the law. Florida law specifically prohibits the transfer of private property to a private developer through the use of eminent domain. It is our contention that this project is not designed for the *public good*."

"We'll have more on that story tonight at 9 PM," the investigative reporter said.

"They're trying to take my goddamn home!" Harlan said.

"Who?" I asked.

"The damn city. They're going to take the land and sell it to a developer who's going to put a resort there. *Public good* my ass! Oh sure, they say it will bring in more tourists, and more money, into the area. We got too many damn tourists already!"

"Can't you fight it?"

"Believe me, I'm trying. That's been my home for 30 years.

I've got no desire to move. They could pay me double what it's worth, I still don't want to move."

Listening to his story made my blood boil. Florida had strict laws to protect against this kind of abuse, but somehow the City Council had deemed the project an acceptable use of eminent domain. They were required to fairly compensate the property owners and provide relocation assistance and funds. But it didn't seem right that someone could come in and snatch your property against your will.

Harlan said he had an attorney. The state was obligated to cover the costs of legal fees to property owners. The state would also cover the cost of an independent appraiser, but no amount of compensation would satisfy Harlan.

He wanted to keep his ocean view.

Even residents that weren't directly affected were pissed about the project. They didn't want a high-rise resort going up in front of their views. They didn't want the increased traffic and congestion that a large resort would bring to the area.

I listened to Harlan bitch for a while. It was just about all he could do at the moment.

I finished my sandwich, said goodbye to Harlan, and strolled down the dock to the *Wild Tide*. Despite the grim circumstances of the morning, it was shaping up to be a nice day—72°, not a cloud in the sky, and a gentle breeze.

It would have been a great day to take the boat out, catch a few rays, do a little fishing, but none of that would happen. Sheriff Daniels called me about the time I entered the salon. "We have ourselves a homicide!"

My face tightened.

"Brenda matched the dental records with Glenn Parker. She found 2, 9mm slugs in his thoracic cavity. I think it's pretty safe to say he didn't drown."

"Does she know when it happened?"

"There's some microbe growing in the flesh. I can't remember what she called it. Anyway, based on its rate of growth, she's estimating it at 36 to 48 hours."

"That's a pretty wide window of opportunity."

"What do you want from me?" Sheriff Daniels said, dryly. "I notified his wife. I want you to head over there and ask her a few questions."

"She's going to love that," I said with a dose of sarcasm.

"Try not to sound like you're interrogating her."

"Do you think she's a suspect?"

"You know the drill. Spouses are always suspects. Glenn was partners with Rick Lowden. They ran a charter business—fishing, diving, etc. See what you can find out. Keep me in the loop."

"Will do," I said.

Daniels gave me the wife's address and the marina where Glenn's boat was docked, as well as Rick Lowden's address.

I caught a cab over to Glenn Parker's residence. It was a modest one-story home with a white picket fence and a nice porch with a bench swing. I knocked on the door and announced myself as a Deputy Sheriff.

Three small yappy dogs bolted toward the door, barking. Their paws clattered against the hardwood floors. I could hear them jumping up and down, scratching at the door, excitedly.

A few moments later, a woman pulled open the door, and scooped the Jack Russell Terriers into her arms. She held a little puppy back with her leg, trying to keep it from bolting into the yard. Her eyes were puffy and red from crying. She had a round face, straight brown hair, and a hint of freckles across her cheeks.

"Mrs. Parker?" I asked over the barking dogs.

She nodded, trying her best to contain the rambunctious animals.

I introduced myself, and the Jack Russells kept barking.

"Stop that," Mrs. Parker said to the dogs.

They didn't listen.

"What are their names?"

"This is Max," she said, nodding to one. "And this is Lucy. And the little one is Buddy."

"Hey Max," I said, extending my hand to pet his head.

A few scratches behind the ear, and underneath the chin, and Max and I were on good terms. Not to be ignored, I gave Lucy an equal amount of affection, then squatted down and petted Buddy.

"I'm sorry about that. They always get excited around new people."

"I'm very sorry for your loss, Mrs. Parker."

"Debbie," she said, correcting my formality.

I stood up. "I know this is a delicate time, but I was wondering if I could ask you a few questions? The sooner I get information, the better chance we have of solving this."

Her face crinkled. "Solving this?"

"Sheriff Daniels didn't tell you?"

She shook her head.

"It looks like your husband was murdered."

She burst into sobs.

The dogs whimpered and licked her face.

I frowned, feeling helpless. I never liked to see people suffer —unless, of course, they deserved it.

After a moment she pulled herself together and invited me in.

I stepped inside, and she led me into the living room and offered me a seat on the couch. She set the dogs down, and they both rushed me.

The interior was tidy, yet lived in. The accommodations were modest. There was a nice 42 inch flatscreen TV and new-ish leather couches that had seen a little wear and tear from the Jack Russells gnawing around the edges.

Max climbed on the couch beside me and nosed his snout under my hand, looking for more affection. Buddy was too short to get on the couch, so I helped him up. He was absolutely adorable, with a white coat and a rusty patch that covered one eye.

Lucy hopped onto the couch and tried to squeeze her way in.

"Need a dog?" Mrs. Parker asked.

"Oh, no! I can barely take care of myself."

"I've given all the little ones away, except Buddy. He could use a good home."

I continued to pet the little guy as I proceeded with my line of inquiry. "When was the last time you saw Glenn?"

Mrs. Parker thought about it for a moment. "Last Thursday, I think. I left town to go visit my mother in Fort Lauderdale. I got back to Coconut Key on Tuesday. Glenn wasn't here. I knew something was wrong right away. I called the sheriff on Wednesday to report him missing."

"How did you know something was wrong?"

"Glenn had left food out on the counter. It had been there a few days. There were roaches in the sink. It freaks me out just thinking about them." She shivered. "Glenn would never leave food out or dirty dishes in the sink. He wasn't a neat freak, but he was clean."

"Were you two having difficulty?"

She hesitated a moment, shifted in her seat, then nodded. "Why do you ask?"

"I noticed you aren't wearing your wedding ring."

She glanced to her hand and frowned, looking embarrassed. There was a small tan line where her ring had been. She took a deep breath. "I'd gone to my mother's to cool off for a few days. I told him I wanted a divorce. We were fighting a lot."

"About what?"

She looked at me like I was prying too much. She hesitated a moment, then answered. "What do couples fight about?"

"Usually money, sex, infidelity..."

She frowned again. "There you go."

"Was he having an affair?" I asked.

Mrs. Parker cringed. "No. I was."

I raised a curious eyebrow.

"I hope you don't think bad of me, it's just that... Glenn had grown distant. I met someone who made me feel pretty and happy, and one thing led to another."

"I understand. These things happen." I paused. "You said you were in a fight. Were the fights ever violent? Did you ever threaten one another?"

"Oh no," she said quickly. "Nothing like that. He was never violent or abusive toward me."

"What about you toward him?"

Her face crinkled. "No. I would never hurt him!" She paused, thinking. "You don't think that I...?"

"No. I'm just trying to get information."

She breathed a sigh of relief.

"Do you own a gun?" I asked, delicately.

Mrs. Parker tightened up again. "Not really. I mean, they're not mine. Glenn has a few hunting rifles, and a few pistols."

"Are they in the house?"

She nodded.

"Do you mind if I take a look at them?"

She hesitated a moment, then stammered, "I guess."

She didn't move for a moment, then she stood from the chair and led me into the bedroom. She opened the closet door and two long rifles were leaning in the corner—a 30.06, and a .270.

"The pistols are in the nightstand on the right side of the bed."

I moved across the room and pulled open the drawer. There was a Smith & Wesson .38 special. It was in pristine condition with nice bluing. Next to it was a 9mm Sig.

I dug in my pocket and pulled out a pair of nitrile gloves. I snapped the purple things on my hands, then picked up the 9mm. I sniffed the weapon and my nose filled with the smell of gun oil and the faint traces of gunpowder.

The weapon hadn't been fired recently.

I press-checked the weapon.

There was a cartridge in the chamber. I pressed the mag release button and dropped out the magazine and inspected it.

It was full.

I slapped it back into the mag well. "Do you mind if I take

this down to the station for analysis? I will return it as soon as we're done."

She froze.

"It will help us rule you out as a suspect. If the ballistics don't match, then this is not the murder weapon."

She relaxed a bit. "Sure, go ahead. I've got nothing to hide." She paused. "For the record. I didn't kill him."

"I'm not suggesting you did. This is just routine procedure."

"Do I need a lawyer?"

"You are within your rights to seek the advice of counsel. But right now you're not a suspect."

"Oh, okay," she said, hesitantly.

"Can you think of anyone who wanted to harm your husband?"

4

"He's had more than a few death threats," Mrs. Parker said

That piqued my curiosity. "From whom?"

"It's total bullshit," she said. "I really feel sorry for the man, but it wasn't Glenn's fault. A former client filed a wrongful death suit. His wife drowned on a deep dive, and he tried to blame Glenn. Said the equipment was faulty." Her face crinkled up. "The equipment wasn't faulty. Glenn was meticulous about caring for his equipment. The truth is, they were diving deeper than they should have been, and the girlfriend freaked out, panicked, and burned through her oxygen. They stayed down too long, and she didn't do the required safety stops on the way up."

"What happened with the lawsuit?"

"It was thrown out. But Nick Phelps continues to blame Glenn. I mean, if anybody's got a motive, it's Nick."

"You know where I can find him?"

"I'm sure I have his contact information around here some-where with all the court papers."

"Can you think of anybody else that might have animosity toward your husband?"

She sighed. "Well, he wasn't getting along too well with his partner, Rick." She paused for a moment in thought. "Where did you say the body was found again?"

"About a mile north of Urchin Key Island."

"Glenn was found at sea. Maybe Rick finally snapped. I would definitely look into him."

"What was the issue?"

"A partnership is like a marriage. There can often be friction over finances."

"How is the business doing?"

"Not well. The lawsuit, and the bad press, really slowed things down. Glenn had a lot of good features, but marketing wasn't one of them. I told him he needed to update his website. It looked like something from 1994. He should have been advertising on social media. I don't know how to do any of that stuff, or I would have helped."

"Did they ever argue?"

"All the time. They started out as friends, but it had gotten to the point where they couldn't stand each other."

"Did Rick ever threaten Glenn?"

She thought for a moment. "Not that I know of."

I thanked her for her time and told her I'd be in touch.

"Are you sure you don't want a dog?" she asked. "He's absolutely adorable."

I grinned. "Thanks, but—"

"Take him for a day. If it doesn't work out, bring him back tomorrow."

"I don't know the first thing about puppies," I said.

Almost on cue, Buddy pawed at my leg and looked at me with his adorably cute eyes. His brow knitted together, looking sad and pathetic.

How could I say no to a face like that?

The dog clearly wielded some type of sorcery that I didn't understand. I was ready to scoop him up and bring him home, but I thought better of it. I didn't have any food or supplies, and I didn't know how JD would feel about a little dog running around, raising hell on his new boat. I didn't even know if the boat would be puppy proof.

"I'll think about it."

"When you're ready, let me know," she said with a used car salesman's grin.

I knelt down and petted Buddy again. I needed to get out of there before I came home with a dog. They all followed me to the door, and I said goodbye.

I was a cold, calculated killer. At least, that's what I kept telling myself. Yet the little puppy was making me feel like a big softy.

Never get emotionally involved with suspects, victims, or clients.

But I already had a soft spot for the dog.

I dropped Parker's 9mm off at the crime lab and headed to *Sea Point Harbor*. I tried to clear my head along the way. I did *not* need a pet—that was for certain.

Sea Point wasn't as nice or as well-maintained as the marina at *Diver Down*, or even *Pirates' Cove*. It was on the west side of the island and was home to several sport-fish charters and commercial fishing operations. The grounds were a little overgrown, and there wasn't a restaurant/bar on the premises.

I strolled down the dock, looking for Glenn's boat, *Moby Debt*. It was a 55' *Ultramarine Sportfish*. She had aggressive styling with a deep-V hull that allowed the boat to carve through the water with ease. The cockpit had a teak deck, tuna door, and live bait well at centerline. The mezzanine had seating for four, with a freezer underneath, and tackle stowage to port.

Floating the monthly note on a boat like this while business was in decline would make just about anyone nervous.

Rick was in the cockpit cleaning up. He was in his early 40s, curly reddish-brown hair, short beard, and a belly that had seen its share of light beer.

A deckhand assisted. He was a skinny guy, sleeved in tattoos, wearing a white tank top and jeans. He had dark hair and dark eyes and didn't seem like he had much experience on a boat.

I flashed my badge and introduced myself.

The two of them exchanged a glance. They didn't look

happy to see me. Or maybe Rick knew I was the bearer of bad news?

"Glenn's dead, isn't he?" Rick said.

"What makes you think that?"

"He's been missing since Tuesday, and you're here investigating. Doesn't take a rocket scientist." Rick sighed, and a grim look washed over his face.

"When was the last time you saw him?" I asked.

"Monday. We had a charter. A couple from Arizona. They wanted to dive the reefs, take some pictures. I can give you their names if you'd like to speak with them."

I nodded.

"We didn't have anything booked Tuesday. Wednesday he didn't show up, and I started to get concerned. In all the time I've known him, he's never been late, much less missed a booking. I called Debbie, and she said she was going to file a missing person's report. That was the last I heard of it until you showed up. What happened?"

"A fishing trawler found his body about a mile north of Urchin Key."

His eyes widened. "No shit?"

"No shit."

"Do you know what happened? I mean, how the hell did he get way out there?"

"I was hoping you might be able to tell me."

"Like I said, I hadn't seen him since Monday." He paused,

processing the information. "Was this some type of accident?"

"Not unless somebody accidentally put 2, 9 mm rounds into his chest."

Rick's eyes widened again. He swallowed hard. "What the fuck?"

"You know anybody who would want to kill Glenn?"

Rick took a deep breath. "I mean, I wanted to strangle the guy at times, but..." he exhaled, thought for a moment, then frowned and shook his head. "You talked to Debbie, I assume?"

I nodded.

"I don't think she's got it in her to do anything, but you can never be too careful. The only guy that I can think of that really had it in for Glenn was the guy that sued us. Nick Phelps. Real piece of work."

"I would assume that Nick Phelps wasn't a fan of yours either?"

"I wasn't there when the incident happened. I was up in Fort Lauderdale at the time. Glenn felt he could manage it by himself."

"So, Nick blamed Glenn exclusively?"

Rick shrugged. "I guess. But who can say what goes on in another man's mind."

5

"What about you?" I asked the deckhand. "Did you know Glenn?"

"This is Carlos," Rick said, introducing us. "I just hired him on a temporary basis. I needed someone to fill in. We've got a client this afternoon."

Carlos nodded and said nothing.

"Today's his first day." Rick smiled. "He's learning the ropes."

"What did you do Monday night after you finished with your client?" I asked Rick.

"I went home, had dinner, drank a few beers, watched Netflix, and spent time with my wife."

"What about Tuesday?"

"If you want to stop by the house and talk with my wife, you're more than welcome. She had me doing *Honey-Dos* around the house all day. *Honey, do this. Honey, do that.*" He frowned. "If you're looking at me as a person of interest, you're barking up the wrong tree. I didn't kill Glenn."

I paused. "Do you own a 9mm?"

"Hell no. .45 ACP!" He puffed up his chest with pride. "Now that's a real man's gun."

"I heard business wasn't doing too good."

"I'm not gonna lie, it's a little tough right now. I had talked to Glenn about selling the boat and closing the business. We're 50-50 partners." Rick sighed. "*Were* 50-50. Glenn was kind of stubborn. He didn't want to let this thing go. It was a dream of his, and he wasn't about to let it die."

Rick's eyes misted a little as he glanced around the boat.

"Now that he's gone, I feel obligated to carry on the dream," Rick said. "Which is a little ironic, I know." He paused for a moment. "Hell, at this point I wouldn't know what else to do. I can't go back and get a regular job after doing this. I don't think I could ever sit behind a desk?"

"I understand that," I said. "Carlos, what's your last name?"

He hesitated a moment then glanced to Rick before addressing me. "Ramirez."

Carlos fidgeted and avoided making eye contact.

"Ever been on a boat before?"

Carlos shook his head.

"Nervous about going out on the water?"

"I can't swim, so... hopefully we don't sink."

There were chuckles all around.

"We won't sink," Rick assured.

"Just don't fall overboard," I cautioned.

An almost imperceptible sneer curled on Carlos's lips.

"You don't like cops much, do you?"

Carlos look surprised by the question. He stammered, "No offense, sir. But my brother was shot by a cop in Dade County. Most cops are just criminals with a free pass."

That hung in the air for a moment, and Rick looked at him like he was crazy for saying it.

"I don't mean no offense. It's just my experience."

I didn't take offense. "There are good cops, and there are bad cops, my friend."

"Maybe. But I've yet to meet a good one," he said.

Now I was mildly offended.

I smiled. "Have a good afternoon, gentlemen."

I gave Rick my information. "If you think of anything that might be useful, get in touch."

"Roger that, chief."

I thanked him for his time, started down the dock, and called an Uber. On the way back to *Diver Down*, JD called.

"What's the word?" I asked.

"Scarlett took the plea deal. We're settling up things now, then we'll grab something to eat, and head back to Coconut

Key. I know one thing for sure, she better keep her happy ass out of trouble."

Neither one of us were holding our breath.

"Well, tell her I'm sorry about the outcome, but it's better than the alternative."

"I will. She's not much in the mood to hear anything right now. Anything developing there?"

I caught him up to speed on all the details, and he said he'd touch base when he got back in town.

The Uber dropped me off at *Diver Down*. It was *Beer:30 PM*, so I strolled inside and sat at the bar.

I ordered, and Madison pulled a long neck from the tub of ice and did her twisty-top maneuver with the bottle opener. Wisps of cool air wafted from the mouth of the bottle. I took a long pull, and the cold beverage tasted good.

I hadn't heard from Isabella since Monaco, and that was probably a good thing. She was still pissed off at me about the fiasco there, and the fact that I had lost Cartwright. He was still on the loose and living the high life.

Cobra Company would catch up to him at some point. If it wasn't me, another operative would take him out.

The organization had a long memory.

You couldn't double-cross an agent and leave him for dead and expect to get away with it. But that's exactly what he had done.

Cartwright had eluded Cobra Company's wrath for longer than I had expected.

I was sort of ambivalent about the whole thing, and I was the one who got shot. But, killing Cartwright wasn't going to change anything that had happened. At the very least, it opened my eyes. And maybe, in a strange way, I should thank him. There was, however, a little matter that I needed to talk to Isabella about.

I reluctantly dialed her number.

"What do you need?" she asked, perturbed.

"I just called to see how you were doing," I said, putting a smile in my voice.

"You're a better liar than that, Tyson," Isabella said, seeing straight through my bullshit. "What do you want?"

"Well, it's been a while now, and all of my accounts are still frozen. You were supposed to be doing something about that. I'm one of the good guys, remember?"

"I put in a request. I don't know why it's taking so long."

"You have explained to our friends at the agency that what happened in Mexico is not my fault?"

"Yes, Tyson. You wouldn't be enjoying the freedoms you now have otherwise."

"So, I'm square with everyone?"

"All of our clients, at least."

Our clients were the big, three-letter agencies.

"So, what's the issue?" I asked.

"I'll check into it," she grumbled, annoyed,

"You and I both know I have a considerable amount of funds in those accounts. I can't even access my numbered account in Switzerland." I paused. "I'm not even sure how anyone else knew about that one."

"Do you think I don't know exactly what my operatives are up to?"

"Cartwright sure caught you by surprise," I quipped.

I could almost hear her nostrils flare at that one.

She paused for a long moment. "I guess it's a good thing that you called. I have another assignment for you."

"Nope. I'm not doing anything until my account situation gets squared away."

"I'll remember that the next time you need something from me." She hung up the phone.

It left me with an uneasy feeling in my gut. As much as I had been trying to get away from my dealings with Cobra Company, I just couldn't seem to break free.

The company had vast resources, a wide network of operatives, and an unrestricted ability to take action. I'm sure, somewhere, there was some type of oversight. There had to be a secret intelligence committee in Congress that had some kind of leverage over the agency, but I wasn't sure.

For all intents and purposes, Cobra Company didn't exist. It operated outside the law at the behest of the government, doing all the little dirty deeds they couldn't, or wouldn't do. But the agency had grown to a massive size and had acquired unimaginable funds. They shaped geopolitics in ways that were incomprehensible. Elected officials only dreamed of having this kind of power.

The tail was certainly wagging the dog.

After I hung up with Isabella, I called Sheriff Daniels.

"What did you find out?" he barked.

"I need you to run a background check on Carlos Ramirez. I also need an address for Nick Phelps. And, I need you to pull up financial transactions, insurance policies, anything that may be relevant to this case."

"See, now this is where I think you're confused. That kind of stuff is not in my job description. That's in your job description."

I frowned. "But I thought my job description was to kick ass and take names?"

Well, you can log into the system and run background checks yourself. Then you can call all the insurance companies and see if they brokered a policy covering Glenn Parker."

"I don't think that's the best use of my time," I said.

Sheriff Daniels growled. "I will put Denise on it."

"Thank you."

"But don't get too *buddy-buddy* with her. The last thing I need is you doing the horizontal mambo with one of my staff."

"Please. I know how to keep professional boundaries."

Daniels chuckled.

Besides, I've never met the girl. Is she hot?"

"I'm quite certain you would not find her attractive."

"Then why did you mention it in the first place?" I had a sneaking suspicion Denise was hot as fuck.

"I don't have time for this. I actually have work to do."

"Right," I said, sarcastically.

Daniels hung up.

I finished my beer and strolled back to the *Wild Tide*. I grabbed another beer and climbed up to the skydeck and took in the view of the marina. I pulled out my phone and started googling how to take care of a puppy.

I thought it might be nice to have a first mate.

6

"Would you turn that damn racket down!" the crotchety man standing on the dock said.

He wore deck shoes, a navy polo, and cream slacks. He had a round nose, weathered face, and bushy eyebrows. His skin was red from the sun and too many broken capillaries. He was probably in his late 50s, with salt-and-pepper hair that curled out underneath his ball cap.

My face crinkled, and I looked at him like he was crazy. I was listening to Led Zeppelin—and not very loud. I glanced at my watch. "It's 8:30 PM."

"I don't care what time it is. It's disturbing me!"

He had strolled down the dock from a 40' sailboat several slips away. The music couldn't have been more than a murmur inside his cabin, yet he was fit to be tied.

I reached over to the controls and turned the stereo down a notch. "How's that?"

"It's still too loud."

"It's on level II."

He glared at me. "It's disturbing me."

I smiled. "I don't think we've had a chance to meet. I'm Tyson. Would you like a beer? Mixed drink?"

"I don't drink with strangers," he growled.

"Did you just move into the marina?"

"Yes, and I've already got a bad taste in my mouth."

"We've got a really good group here. I'm sure once you settle in, you'll really enjoy the place."

"Not if I have to listen to this noise every night," he grumbled. "I'll give it till 9 o'clock. If I hear this racket after that, I'm calling the cops."

A thin smile curled on my lips. I pulled my gold badge from my pocket and flashed it. "I'll be here waiting on your call."

He snarled at me, then stormed down the dock and climbed aboard his boat.

I chuckled to myself and shook my head. What the hell was Madison thinking renting a slip to this guy?

There was no way he was going to fit in around here. It was a pretty calm place most of the time. But on the weekends, people liked to enjoy themselves with friends and a few drinks. Sometimes the festivities went on into the wee hours of the morning. This was the Keys—you were supposed to have fun. We all chose this life for a little adventure, and the occasional party went with the territory.

JD showed up about 9:30PM and was in need of something to sooth his nerves. "I sure am glad that shit's over!"

He scaled the transom and pushed into the salon. He met me on the skydeck with a glass of whiskey. He took a seat on the settee, and sipped the amber liquid, gasping with satisfaction. "I swear that girl's gonna make me grow old before my time."

"You're already old."

He scowled at me. "You'll get here one day."

"Don't count on it," I said knowing full well my odds of making it to old age were slim, especially with my lifestyle. "How's Scarlett taking it?"

"She thinks her social life is over. And it should be. That's what got her into this mess in the first place." An exasperated breath escaped Jack's mouth. "She's still pretty screwed up about Sadie. Maybe this whole thing will serve as a wake-up call."

We shot the shit on the skydeck for another hour. The full moon hung low in the sky, glimmering across the water. Mr. Miller stormed down the dock and complained once again. Not long after that, I got a call from Sheriff Daniels. "What kind of hell are you two raising now?"

"Let me guess... You got a noise complaint?" I asked.

"Damn right I did."

"The guy is overreacting. I'm sitting here with JD discussing the case."

"Well, keep it down," the sheriff said.

"Can you hear my stereo?"

"No."

"See," I said. "He's just being cranky."

"You guys represent the department. So put on a good front."

"That's asking a little much, don't you think?" I muttered, my voice thick with sarcasm.

"From you two? That's asking a whole lot!" Daniels hung up the phone.

"I've got a string of firecrackers in the trunk," JD said. "What say we light those bastards off about 3 AM?"

The idea was tempting.

Jack was serious.

"No need to pull out the heavy artillery just yet," I cautioned.

We had another beer, then JD made his way home. I climbed down from the skydeck and curled in bed in the master stateroom.

The next morning I made a trip to the pet store and stocked up on supplies.

I must have been out of my mind.

I picked up some premium puppy food, a stainless steel water bowl, a collar, a name tag, a 6' leash, a dog brush, shampoo, toothpaste, a tooth brush, a few chew toys, flea and tick control, nail clippers, and a crate. No trip to the pet store would be complete without doggy treats.

I brought the loot back to the boat and started puppy-proofing the vessel. I figured Buddy could have the VIP guest suite all to himself. Of course, I'd have to get Madison to look after him while we were on charters, but I figured she wouldn't mind.

Especially after she saw him.

I called Debbie Parker, and told her I'd like to take Buddy off her hands. But the response I got, surprised me.

7

"I'm sorry," Debbie said, her voice crackling through my phone. "I already gave him away. A friend of mine called after you left and said she'd take him. Should have grabbed him while you had the chance."

I tried to ignore the deep sense of disappointment that twisted in my stomach. "It's no big deal. It's probably for the best, anyway."

"I'm sorry you couldn't be Buddy's forever home."

"I'm sure he found a good one."

"Have you made any progress on the case? Can you clear me as a suspect yet?"

"I don't have any new information at this time. I'm sorry."

I thanked her for her time and hung up. A frowned pulled my face, still trying to pretend I wasn't disappointed. I figured I would take all the supplies back in the afternoon.

Denise, from the Sheriff's Office, called. "I have the information you requested."

I lifted a surprised eyebrow. "Really? That was quick."

"It wasn't hard," she said with a cheery, bubbly voice.

She gave me the address for Nick Phelps who was living in Miami. "It looks like there was a life insurance policy worth $2 million, with Brenda Parker named as the primary beneficiary."

"That would certainly provide a motive for murder."

"Well, if you like that, you're going to love this. Moby Debt, LLC had a life insurance policy on its principles. If either of the members died, the surviving partner would be the primary beneficiary of the $4 million policy."

She let that hang there for a moment.

"I think that would solve Rick Lowden's financial problems."

"Multiple suspects with multiple motives... Looks like you've got your work cut out for you."

I agreed. "Anything from the crime lab yet?"

"No, but I will be sure to call you as soon as I find out anything. Oh, Carlos Ramirez... felony B&E, felonious assault. Out on parole."

"I appreciate you doing this."

"No problem," she said.

I pictured a cute face to go along with the friendly voice.

"It's my job," she continued. "That's what I'm here for. Let me know if you need anything else."

"I will."

I hung up and called JD. I told him we needed to make a trip to Miami to interview Nick Phelps.

"Is the county gonna pay for the gas?" JD asked.

Judging by the size of the boat JD just bought, I didn't think he was hurting for cash. But then again, maybe he was? It was a helluva purchase.

"Quit your bitching," I said. "Save your receipts."

"I've got a few things to take care of, then I'll swing by and pick you up."

"Oh, shit! We've got the Gala tonight," I remembered. "We'll never make it back in time."

"It would be a good excuse not to go to the gala," JD said, throwing it out there.

"Daniels was pretty firm about that being mandatory. We can run up there tomorrow."

"No can do. We've got a charter tomorrow."

"Really?"

"Yes, really. That boat ain't going to pay for itself. Well, it will... but not if we keep passing up charters." He paused. "What time is this event tonight."

"7PM."

"I'll pick you up at 6:30," JD said before hanging up.

A cheeseburger was calling my name, so I strolled down the dock to *Diver Down* and took a seat at the bar. Madison occupied her time with Ryan. She giggled and doted on him. It was enough to elicit an eye roll.

After I cleared my throat exaggeratedly, she came over and took my order. "What will it be?"

"Cheeseburger. Cheddar. Sweet potato fries."

"I'll take another beer," Harlan said. "Or should I go to *Pirates' Cove*?"

Madison dug into a tub of ice, pulled out a long neck, and popped the top. She slid it across the counter to Harlan and said, "This one's on the house."

"What's Ryan's last name?" I asked.

"Johnson, why?" Her eyes narrowed at me, realizing why I asked. "Do NOT do a background check on him."

I shrugged innocently. "I was just curious. That's all. Besides, I've got enough things to do. I don't have time to look into your new boyfriend."

She rolled her eyes. "You don't seem very busy to me."

"A lot of my work is cerebral. I may not look busy, but I'm constantly analyzing," I said, laying it on thick.

"Don't hurt yourself. I guess since you're *working* right now you won't be drinking beer." She poured a Diet Coke and slid it across the bar.

She sent my order back to the kitchen and resumed flirting with Ryan.

"How's it going, Harlan?" I asked.

"Same shit, different day."

That was the extent of our conversation.

A trailer for Bree Taylor's new movie played on the television. My heart felt heavy. She appeared breathtaking on the screen, and I think my heart stopped for a moment.

"Is it true you banged her?" Harlan asked.

I gave him a sideways glance. "We had a brief, but meaningful relationship."

A sly grin curled on Harlan's craggy lips.

Madison's service may have gone downhill, but the food was still great. The burger was thick and juicy. I scarfed it down like I'd been on a desert island for days.

Afterward, I sat at the bar for a while, contemplating the case and mustering the motivation to return the pet supplies. It dawned on me that tonight's gala was a black-tie affair and I had nothing to wear.

I settled my tab and darted out of the bar. I went back to the boat and grabbed a wad of cash from my poker winnings, then caught an Uber to the Highland Village Mall. I picked up a black *Biagi* suit, tuxedo shirt, tie and cumber bun, along with a pair of *Cipriani* black leather lace-up shoes. I grabbed a few *De Fiore* slim cut dress shirts for good measure. I could mix-and-match them with the suit when needed.

It came to the tidy sum of $2395. A little bit more than I had planned on spending, but hey, the suit fit well.

Dress to impress.

The suit came with a thin garment cover, and the clerk gave

me a bag for the shoes and dress shirts. I strolled through the open-air mall to the parking lot and fumbled for my phone. As I was calling for a ride, I felt the cold steel barrel of a weapon press against the back of my skull.

A gruff voice shouted, "Give me your wallet and drop the bags!"

8

I t was a stupid mistake.

I had my head in my phone and should have had better situational awareness. But I didn't think anybody would be stupid enough to try to mug me in broad daylight!

This jackass was in for a rude awakening.

I slowly unslung the suit from my shoulder and set it, and the shopping bag, on the sidewalk.

Faster than a jackrabbit on crack, I sidestepped, twisted around, grabbed the barrel of the weapon and shoved it skyward.

My elbow slammed into the man's nose, splattering blood into his ski mask. I twisted the barrel around 180° and stripped the weapon.

My knee smacked his balls, and the thug doubled over with a groan.

I planted my elbow into his spine and dropped him to the sidewalk, then kicked him in the ribs for good measure.

For the next two weeks, every time he took a breath, he'd remember the mistake he'd made.

Cracked ribs suck.

"Deputy Sheriff! You're under arrest, scumbag!"

I slipped a pair of handcuffs from a cargo pocket and ratcheted them around his wrists. Then I pulled the ski mask off his head.

He was maybe 25 and looked strung out. His face was broken out, and his cheeks were drawn from too much methamphetamine. I figured his addiction led him to make poor life choices, committing unthought out crimes to feed his addiction.

I called the station, and the sheriff arrived in a patrol car a few minutes later. We hoisted the perp off the sidewalk and stuffed him into the back of the squad car.

"This is all your fault, you know?" I said.

Sheriff Daniels flashed me a quizzical look.

"I wouldn't have been here if it weren't for the gala."

"Then somebody else would have gotten mugged, and this perp would still be on the street."

"So, you're saying I should get some sort of commendation?" I said with a grin.

He stared at me flatly.

I grabbed my bags from the sidewalk and climbed into the

passenger seat and rode with Daniels back to the station. I spent an hour writing an incident report. I liked the *chasing bad guys* part.

Not so much on the paperwork.

I was in a conference room, sitting in a black leather IKEA chair at an oval mahogany table, scribbling out details. The sound of keyboards clacking and phones ringing filtered down the corridor.

Denise poked her head in through the open door. "You're Tyson, right?"

I looked up from my chicken scratch to see the best looking deputy I'd ever seen. It was hard to make the polyester uniform look sexy, but Denise did a fine job. She had red hair, green eyes, and creamy skin.

I could instantly see what Sheriff Daniels was worried about.

She stepped into the room with her arm outstretched and we shook hands. Her skin was soft, but her grip was firm. "I'm Denise. It's so good to put a face to the name. I've heard so much about you and JD."

I cringed. "Uh, oh."

She smiled. "It's not all bad."

"Just mostly bad?"

She laughed. "I don't think Sheriff Daniels would keep you two around if you didn't provide some benefit. I haven't known him very long, but I get the impression he doesn't suffer fools lightly."

"I guess he's making an exception in our case," I said in a self-deprecating way.

"Well, I've got to get back to work. It was nice to meet you. Will I see you at the gala tonight?"

"Absolutely."

She left the conference room, leaving subtle traces of her presence lingering in the air—some type of scented body wash.

It wasn't overpowering, but enough to make me want to investigate further.

I had to tell myself that she was off-limits. Sheriff Daniels was understandably concerned about the potential complications of interdepartmental romances in the current culture.

I finished the report under the pale florescent light, feeling like I was back in school. I turned in my essay and headed back to the *Wild Tide* to get ready for the evening's event.

The tuxedo fit perfect.

I didn't have much occasion to dress up in Coconut Key. It was mostly T-shirts and shorts.

The howl of the flat six filtered through the marina as JD pulled his red Porsche into the parking lot of *Diver Down*. My phone buzzed a moment later.

"I'm here," JD said. "Hurry your ass up."

"I am *Oscar Mike*."

I slipped the phone into my pocket and made a few last-minute adjustments to my bowtie in front of the mirror. I moved down the companionway and climbed the stairs to the salon and pushed into the cockpit. The orange sun hung low in the sky, and a cool breeze coming off the water ruffled my hair. The marina looked like it belonged on a postcard. Waves lapped against the hull, and the boats gently rocked on the water.

I glanced down to Mr. Miller and waved.

He sat in the cockpit of this boat, enjoying the evening with a sandwich and a beer.

He didn't wave back.

He just stared at me with a cold gaze and a quizzical look, probably wondering what the hell I was doing wearing a tuxedo. Most people came to Coconut Key so they'd never have to put on a suit again.

I climbed over the transom and strolled down the dock. A chuckle escaped my lips when I saw JD and his idea of formal attire.

9

"This is supposed to be *black-tie*," I said.

A scowl crinkled on JD's face. "This is *black tie*, bitch!"

With the top down and the music blaring, JD sat in his midlife crisis, wearing a tuxedo jacket, loud Hawaiian shirt, black bowtie, beige cargo shorts, and checkered vans sneakers. He had his long hair pulled back in a ponytail and wore dark Ray Bans.

I climbed into the car and pulled the door shut.

JD dropped the car into gear, let out the clutch, and gravel spit as we peeled out of the parking lot.

I shouted over the wind and music, "I don't think Sheriff Daniels is going to be too happy about your attire."

"What's he going to do? Fire us?"

I shrugged.

JD may not have been a rock star, but he wasn't aware of that fact.

We raced across the island to the *Seven Seas Hotel* and pulled to the valet stand. JD hopped out of the car and tossed the keys to the attendant and kept walking. "Put it someplace nice."

The *Seven Seas* was a five-star luxury hotel on the water. It offered stunning views, a private marina, and a relaxing pool with several bars, grilled food, and plenty of eye candy.

Tonight, the pool area was home to the gala.

We strolled through the opulent lobby and made our way poolside. A number of guests had already arrived and were milling about, drinking free cocktails, and socializing. A number of silent auction items were on display, and guests perused the merchandise. It had all been donated in an effort to raise money for pediatric cancer patients—a worthy cause, no doubt.

My eyes scanned the area, looking for Sheriff Daniels, but they got stuck on a sultry redhead in a black strapless evening gown that shimmered when she moved.

She had smooth, aggressive styling with all the factory options installed. The strapless gown accentuated her elegant shoulders and toned back. Her waist tapered to a slim hourglass figure, and her backside could wake the dead. Her hair was styled to perfection, and she looked like a classic movie star from a bygone era.

When she spun around, I realized I was staring at Denise.

She saw me, and her green eyes brightened. She waved from across the pool.

JD was equally as mesmerized as I was. "Who the hell is that?"

"She's off-limits."

"What, are you calling dibs?"

"No. I mean, she's off-limits. She's a new deputy."

"I'm certainly going to have to break the law now," JD muttered. "She could handcuff me anytime."

We strolled over to greet her, and I introduced JD. He did his best not to let his eyes get distracted by her mesmerizing form.

"I like your tux," she said to JD.

He had garnered more than a fair share of disapproving stares from the guests.

"Thank you," JD responded with a smile, then replied in kind. "That is a beautiful gown."

She beamed. "Thank you."

I could see an inappropriate comment swirling behind JD's eyes. I decided to change the subject. "Denise is really efficient at gathering information."

"I bet. She's probably really good at a lot of things."

She smiled. "It just took a few phone calls and a friendly voice."

"Well, you've certainly got that," I said.

"Where's the sheriff?" JD asked.

"I haven't seen him yet," Denise said, glancing around. "Oh, there he is!"

The sheriff just entered the pool area and was smiling and shaking hands as he made his way through the crowd. He was already campaigning for re-election.

"There's an open bar," Denise said. "You guys help yourselves."

"Don't mind if I do," JD said.

Denise excused herself and continued to mingle.

We strolled over to a hut with a thatched roof and ordered top shelf liquor. The bartender poured two glasses of whiskey and slid them across the counter. I put a healthy tip in his glass jar which was mostly empty, despite the affluent clientele.

I took a sip of the whiskey and watched as more people began to trickle into the event. It was a *Who's Who* of Coconut Key—socialites with money to burn. It was an occasion for them to make an appearance, be seen, and throw money at a good cause.

JD and I perused the auction items. There was a guitar signed by Eddie Van Halen. A pair of boxing gloves signed by Mike Tyson. There was a *Go-Fast* boat that had been confiscated from a drug dealer. Items ranged from the affordable to the astronomical. The name of the donor was prominently displayed by each item.

JD slipped in a bid for the guitar.

"I see you got the memo," Sheriff Daniels said in a low growl as he stepped behind us.

JD smiled. "You like the shoes?"

Daniels glared at him. "This is an important event. Everyone here is a potential campaign donor. How's it going to look when I introduce you two as my Special Investigation Unit?"

"We're definitely special, alright," JD boasted.

"You can say that again," the sheriff grumbled, and he didn't mean it as a compliment.

"You've been holding out on us," JD said. "How long has Denise been working with the department?"

Wayne's eyes narrowed. "A few weeks now. And both of you need to keep your hands to yourself. The last thing I need is a harassment suit. Just pretend she's ugly and annoying."

"After three drinks, there are no ugly girls," JD said.

Sheriff Daniels was not amused.

"Okay, okay, lighten up," JD said. "You act like we have no self-control."

Sheriff Daniels rolled his eyes and strolled away.

"There's something so satisfying about annoying him," JD said, lightheartedly.

He took another gulp of his whiskey and swallowed it down. "You ready for another?"

I nodded, and JD strolled back to the bar.

I continued to look over the auction items. There was a weeklong vacation package, donated from the Coconut Key Development Group, LLC. It was an all-inclusive stay at the upcoming resort that was soon to be built where Harlan's house now stood.

My jaw tightened.

"You look upset," a sultry voice said. "Or are you just a generally unpleasant person?"

10

At first I was a little annoyed, and I was fully prepared with a snarky comeback. But the woman had a face to match her smooth, sultry voice, and I found myself disinclined to say anything negative.

She was drop dead gorgeous—tan skin, dark eyes, full lips with deep red lipstick. Her flowing raven hair hung to her shoulders, and a diamond necklace sparkled around her neck. The jewelry drew my eyes to her elegant collarbones and down to her sumptuous cleavage that was barely contained by a strapless gown. It was painted on and hugged her delightful curves. She had elbow-length gloves and a pearl bracelet on her left wrist.

The lavender sky grew dim as the sun sunk low on the horizon. The leaves of palm trees rustled in the wind, and the crowded event was gearing up.

"I'm not upset," I said. "I just get annoyed when scumbag developers push people out of their homes."

She arched a curious eyebrow. "I hear the resort will bring in a substantial amount of extra revenue for the city, and the residents are being handsomely compensated for the move." She paused for a moment. "What brings you here tonight?"

"I'm here like everybody else. To support a good cause."

"Are you one of these super-wealthy entrepreneurs?"

"No. I am... retired. But I volunteer as a deputy sheriff."

She perked up. "Ooh, that sounds intriguing. She leaned in and whispered, "I'm so sick of these rich douche-bags, always trying to impress with their toys. Their fancy cars and big yachts. They're so boring."

"Don't hold it against me, but I do have a big yacht." The subtle double entendre wasn't lost on her.

"I'll bet you do."

In this setting, it seemed fitting to introduce myself as, "Wild, Tyson Wild."

Her silk gloved hand took mine, and we shook.

"Luciana Varga. Scumbag developer," she said with a piercing glance.

I swallowed hard and did a poor job of containing my surprise.

"It's okay. I stick my foot in my mouth all the time."

I forced an uncomfortable smile. I couldn't tell if she was amused or annoyed.

"It was nice to meet you, Mr. Wild. I'm sure I'll see you around."

She drifted away and greeted the Mayor. He seemed pleased to see her—and who wouldn't be?

"Who is that?" JD asked, returning with our drinks.

I finished the last sip of my first drink with a gulp and took the second, finishing it off equally fast. "Trouble."

"I like trouble," JD said with a mischievous glint in his eyes.

We mingled around and had a few more drinks. The event was in full swing.

"I love your outfit," a woman said to JD.

She was serious too!

She was in her 40s and had her hair in an updo, styled to perfection. She wore a white gown with pearls around her neck. She looked elegant and sophisticated. "I wish I had the balls to dress casual to these stuffy events."

"Why, thank you, ma'am." JD replied with a wide smile.

"Oh, please! Don't ma'am me. My name is Helen."

"It's a pleasure to meet you, Helen," JD said.

He introduced us.

"One day I'm tempted to show up to one of these things wearing nothing at all."

"Please let me know when you do," JD said.

She was well put together.

Helen smiled, enjoying the attention. Then she fished for
another compliment. "I'm afraid that might traumatize too
many people."

"I don't know. You don't seem frightening to me."

Her pupils widened and her eyes sparkled. "You are a
charmer, sir."

"I just call them like I see them." JD grinned.

"Looks like your drink is empty. Shall we find the bar?"
Helen suggested.

"We shall."

The two hit it off instantly.

JD and Helen made their way to the bar, her hand clinging
to his arm. He glanced over his shoulder and flashed me an
optimistic grin as he walked away.

I chuckled and shook my head.

The mayor stepped up on a riser and clanked his wine glass
with a spoon. "May I have everyone's attention?"

The crowd settled, and the chatter died down.

"I want to thank you all for coming out this evening. This
cause is very near and dear to my heart. As you all know, my
daughter Maggie lost her fight earlier this year. Every dollar
you spend on the auction this evening will go directly to
pediatric cancer research and treatment programs. The
auctions are silent, so I urge you to bid, and bid high."

There were giggles among the crowd.

Mayor Styles smiled. "And if you don't win your auction,

you are always free to make a direct donation. In that regard, I would like to thank Luciana Varga for the generous contribution made on behalf of the Coconut Key Development Group. In my hand, I am holding a check in the amount of $1 million."

The crowd cheered and clapped as he held the check overhead, flapping it in the breeze.

"I know many of you have a healthy spirit of competition, and I'm sure you don't want to be outdone," the mayor continued.

There was another round of laughter.

"Once again, thank you all for coming, and enjoy the evening!" He stepped down from the riser to another round of applause.

It was an impressive donation. I wondered how much she had privately donated to the mayor's campaign?

Luciana was instantly flocked by other guests, looking to chat her up—many of whom were probably seeking donations to their own foundations.

I waited for the vultures to thin out, then made sure I bumped into Luciana again. "Very generous for a scumbag."

She gave me a dry smile. "What did you think? That I'm some meany that clubs baby seals?"

I looked her up and down. "I don't know. I bet you've got a mean streak."

She arched an eyebrow at me. "Have you been talking to my ex? He'll tell you I've got a little bit of a temper. But I keep it in check most of the time." She shrugged it off. "What can I say? I'm high-performance. Gotta take the good with the bad."

"Obviously there's a lot of good in there, somewhere."

A thin smile curled on her lips. "Don't tell anyone. You'll ruin my reputation."

"Have you met any of the people your project is displacing? I mean, really gotten to know them?"

"Some of them are suing me, trying to get an injunction. So, I've gotten to know their attorneys."

"Some people have built a lot of memories in those homes. Memories that money can't buy."

She sighed. "What if I up my buyout offers and increase my relocation allowance? Would that make you happy?"

"You don't have to make *me* happy."

"I'll have my attorney put in a new settlement offer. One that is more than fair. I really think this project is gonna benefit the community as a whole. You should stop by my office sometime and see the plans."

"I'd like that."

"There you are," Styles said, interrupting us. "I just wanted to thank you again for your kindness and compassion."

Luciana flashed me a prideful look before addressing the mayor. "You're more than welcome. Have you met Tyson Wild?"

"I don't think we've been formally introduced," Styles said.

We shook hands.

"He's a volunteer deputy sheriff."

"Excellent. I appreciate all you do to keep the streets and shores of Coconut Key safe." He smiled a politician's smile. "If you'll excuse me, I have a private matter I'd like to discuss with Miss Varga."

I excused myself and looked around the venue for JD. A text dinged on my phone. "You're on your own. The Eagle has landed. Catch you tomorrow."

Obviously things were progressing well with Helen.

She was about two decades out of his usual target range. I was looking forward to a full *after action* report in the morning.

11

J D showed up bright and early the next morning, fully caffeinated. He stomped on board, making a ruckus, rattling the bulkheads. "Rise and shine, Princess."

I peeled open my eyes, wiped away the sleep, and crawled out of bed.

"You would not believe what happened last night," JD shouted through the hatch.

"I'm sure you'll tell me all about it." I got dressed and staggered up to the salon and started making myself breakfast.

"What the hell is this?" JD asked as his eyes got stuck on a bag of puppy food.

I shrugged, sheepishly. "Madison's getting a puppy."

He didn't ask any further questions, and I left it at that.

"So tell me... How was it?"

A wide grin tugged at JD's lips. "That woman is something

else. First, she's loaded. And when I say loaded, I mean *loaded*. Her ex-husband is some tech billionaire, and she made out like a bandit in the split."

"So, you've got a new sugar mama?"

"Hey now," JD said, taking offense. "I don't need no sugar mama. But it doesn't suck to date rich women."

"So, you're dating now?"

JD shrugged. "We're getting to know each other. We got to know each other really well last night. And let me tell you, that girl has got a body on her. Mmm, mmm. Pilates and plyometrics payoff. She had serious hidden talent under that gown. I mean, I thought I was gonna have a heart attack just trying to keep up."

"Isn't she a little old for you," I said, taunting him.

"Age is just a number. Besides, she gets my references when I mention bands from the 80s."

"Oh. Don't tell me you actually like her?"

"Like I said. We're getting to know each other."

"So, you're going to see her again?"

"I would hope so."

JD reached into his pocket and pulled out a pill bottle. He popped a few hydrocodone into his mouth and washed them down with a swig of bottled water.

I gave him a curious glance. "You're still on those?"

"Just here and there. A little lingering pain from my injury. I was shot, remember? While I was helping you, I might add."

I raised my hands in surrender. "Just checking."

The room was silent a moment.

"How many of those are you taking a day?"

"Just a few."

"Isn't your prescription out?"

"I had to finagle a few extra."

I frowned at him. "You're buying these off the street?"

"Newsflash. There's an opioid crackdown. You know how hard this stuff is to come by?"

I let out a disapproving sigh. "You're a grown man. You can make your own decisions. But I think you should start tapering off those."

"I've only been on them for two weeks now. Lighten up."

I dropped it, but I was growing mildly concerned.

After breakfast, we prepped the boat and filled the tanks. JD planned our course.

Our clients, Ted and Charlotte, were from Texas. They were experienced divers and had said they were looking for a leisurely afternoon of swimming the reefs, taking pictures, and enjoying a little fun in the sun. But they had something else planned when they arrived.

Ted was in his 60s, but didn't look it. He had a full head of deep black hair, and the only traces of gray were specs in his goatee. He had tanned skin, and a gravelly voice. I could tell he used to be a little heavier, but had taken off some weight.

His clothes were slightly baggy. The guy always had a smile on his face.

Charlotte was blonde, maybe 15 years younger. She had gorgeous bone structure and stunning blue eyes. If you met them separately, you'd never figure the two of them as a couple, but together, they seemed to fit perfectly.

Charlotte handed me a specific set of coordinates that pointed to a location just north of Angelfish Key Island.

JD and I exchanged a curious glance.

"Why do you want to go there?" I asked. "There's nothing to see. No reefs. No shipwrecks."

A sly grin curled on Charlotte's lips. "That's where I believe you are wrong."

The couple exchanged a glance that was full of possibilities. There was a secret behind their eyes, and they were contemplating whether to spill the beans. But like all good secrets, they have to escape some time.

"Are you familiar with the *Santa Paquita De Cádiz?*" Charlotte asked.

I shrugged and exchanged a glance with JD, but he didn't know either.

"It's a Spanish galleon. It was in route to Spain in the 1700s and sunk somewhere in the mid Atlantic. It never made it to its destination and has never been found."

"Interesting, but we are nowhere near the mid-Atlantic," I said, stating the obvious.

"Rumor has it the *Santa Paquita* was raided by pirates, and most of her treasure stolen. We believe the pirate ship, the *Black Rose*, sank during a hurricane and is somewhere north of Angelfish Key island."

"I know they pull Spanish gold out of these waters every now and again, but that story seems a little far-fetched, don't you think?" JD said in a doubtful tone.

Charlotte shrugged. "The hunt is half the fun, isn't it?"

I couldn't disagree with her.

"The galleon was said to have been carrying over $500 million worth of gold," Charlotte added.

That was enough to pique my interest.

"I've got a proposition for you," Charlotte said. "How about you take us out and let us dive the area, no charge? In exchange, you get 50% of anything we find? And you keep this whole thing between us."

I looked to JD, and we both contemplated her offer.

12

I t sounded intriguing, and what did we really have to lose?

"Even if you find the *Santa Piña Colada*, you realize the state is going to claim ownership of anything you bring up," JD said. "In the past they've let the salvors keep 75% of the intrinsic value, but there are no guarantees."

"What happens if we don't tell the state?" Charlotte asked.

"Try selling a historic object without raising a few eyebrows," JD said, flatly. "You'll be charged with fraud and countless other felonies. If you find the wreckage, register a claim with the state, and get a contract for the salvage rights."

The prospect hung in the air for a few moments.

"So, what do you say?" Charlotte asked.

JD paused for a long moment. "Let's go hunt some treasure!"

We disconnected the shore power and water, cast off the lines, and Jack took the helm.

The engine burbled as we idled out of the marina. Once we reached open water, Jack throttled up the engines and brought the boat on plane. We raced across the water, carving through the waves like a knife through icing on a cake.

I chatted with Ted and Christine as we made our way to the dive site. "How did you put all this together?"

"I'm a data analyst. My brain sees trends and connections. I read about the demise of the *Santa Paquita* and filed it away in my memory bank somewhere. Then, a year later, I read a memoir written by Jacques De La Fontaine. He was a former commander in the French Navy in the late 1600s. Then he decided to branch out on his own. See, the French actually authorized piracy during that time as a way to harass Spanish and British fleets. He was a dreaded and feared marauder on the water in the Caribbean. When the *Black Rose* went down, he survived with a handful of the crew. They were stranded on an island before being rescued by a merchant vessel. In his book he describes numerous incidents on the high seas. While he didn't specifically mention the *Santa Paquita*, the description, and the timing of events, coincides."

"So this is all speculation on your part?"

"Very well researched speculation."

"Jacques De La Fontaine had amassed an enormous amount of wealth. And he had in his possession a handful of Spanish doubloons that could only have come from the *Santa Paquita*."

I didn't know what to make of her story, but it was interesting, and provided the couple with an adventurous quest. Though, it all seemed like a stretch.

We reached the dive site and dropped anchor. Jack flew the diver down flag, and the couple donned their dive gear.

"Be careful down there, and watch your time," I said. "You're going pretty deep. The depth meter says it's 112 feet. Including your descent, you'll only have a few minutes at the bottom before you'll have to begin your ascent. Don't forget your safety stop."

Charlotte smiled. "I know. This isn't our first rodeo."

The two divers plunged into the water, and bubbles rose to the surface. I took a seat at the settee in the mezzanine.

At the depth they were diving, they'd have to work fast. Once they surfaced, there would be a long surface interval to reduce the nitrogen buildup in their blood.

If nitrogen bubbles form in your bloodstream, you're in a world of hurt, doubled over with the bends. In severe cases, without the proper treatment, it can be fatal.

The tricky thing about diving in greater depths is the stress factors that many people don't often account for. You can be calm, cool, and collected while diving near the surface. In 20 feet of water you can easily reach fresh air on a breath-hold. It becomes a little more challenging at 112 feet. The heightened adrenaline can increase heartbeat and respiration, and a diver can burn through oxygen more quickly than anticipated. Throw in an equipment malfunction, and a leisurely dive becomes a death sentence.

JD joined me in the cockpit and took a seat on the gunwale as the boat gently rocked with the waves.

"We should run up to Miami tomorrow and talk to Nick Phelps," I said. "I was going over Scott Kingston's ledgers. I tracked my parents' boat. It was re-titled and given a new HIN. It's currently registered to Rory Tilman in Miami. I thought we might stop by and ask him a few questions."

"Don't get your hopes up," JD said. "This guy probably has no information about the origin of the vessel. He probably doesn't know the boat was stolen. I'm sure he doesn't know two people were murdered on it."

"Right now, it's the only lead I've got. That, and the initials, XC. That's who sold the boat to Kingston in the first place."

Jack let out a grim sigh. "We'll find out who killed your parents. I promise."

I frowned. "You know the odds with cold cases."

"Fuck the odds."

"If XC didn't kill my parents, maybe he can lead us to who did?"

We sat in silence for a moment.

"I need a beer," JD said. "How long do you think we're into this treasure hunt for?"

I glanced at my watch. "They should be coming up soon. With an hour surface interval, that will put them into pressure group C. Two hours puts them into pressure group A."

A flurry of bubbles rose to the surface, and the divers emerged from the water. They climbed onto the swim platform, and I helped them scale the transom into the cockpit. "Are we rich yet?"

My tongue was planted firmly in my cheek.

Judging by the disappointed looks on their faces I wasn't surprised by their answer.

"We didn't see anything," Charlotte said. "But it doesn't mean it's not nearby somewhere. I'd like to make another trip down."

"I'd recommend against it. With the surface interval of an hour, you're only going to have six minutes of downtime." Better safe than sorry. Neither of you want to get bent."

The couple thought about it for a moment, then agreed. Instead, we took them to a nearby reef where they could make a few more dives in shallow water without compromising their safety.

It was late afternoon by the time we returned to the marina.

"Sorry we didn't find anything," Charlotte said. "We planned a quick trip this vacation, but we would like to come back in a few months. We'll be in touch then."

We said our goodbyes, and JD and I cleaned and stowed the gear.

"I think we just got taken," JD said.

"So do I."

"Oh, well. Live and learn." He glanced to his watch. "I told Ian I'd stop by the *Oceanographic Institute* this afternoon, if I had chance. How about we catch happy hour at *Riptide* afterward?"

"Sounds like a plan."

We left the marina, and JD drove toward the institute.

"Have you ever met Ian?" JD asked.

I shook my head.

"He's a character."

JD was one to talk.

"Kooky son-of-a-bitch, but a lovable guy. "

"What does he want?"

13

The Coconut Key Oceanographic Institute was a private, nonprofit research facility. It was committed to the study of marine science and engineering, focusing on plant, animal, and microbial life in the Keys and South Florida. They were concerned with coastal erosion, pollution, the health of the reefs, and the surrounding sea life.

Despite their nonprofit status, the Institute had designed a number of cutting-edge submersibles, remote operated vehicles, and marine accessories. Most of its funding came from the licensing of these patents to other manufacturers. Despite the local focus, the Oceanographic Institute was involved in activities and expeditions across the globe.

Ian Ainsly was world-renowned in his field.

We pulled into the parking lot, then strolled toward the main building. JD pulled open the glass door and motioned for me to enter.

I nodded, appreciative of his hospitality.

A receptionist sitting behind a counter greeted us. "Welcome, gentlemen. How may I assist you? Are you interested in a tour of the aquarium?"

"No, we're here to see Ian Ainsley," JD said.

"Just one moment."

The receptionist picked up the phone and buzzed Ian's extension. "Mr. Ainsley, there are two gentlemen here to see you. A mister...?"

"Donovan," JD said.

"Wild," I added.

"Donovan and Wild," the receptionist said.

"Yes, sir. Right away, sir," the receptionist said with an urgent tone.

She hung up the phone and pointed down the hallway. "Just through those double doors, then take a left, and the research lab will be on your right."

We smiled at her and followed her directions.

The research lab was a large two-story bay with multiple aquatic tanks that were at least 15x20 and filled with water. There were computer terminals and machining equipment. Raw materials. Prototype products. Rows of storage racks housed every imaginable part. What couldn't be purchased off the shelf could be fabricated with machining equipment and 3D printers. Anything you could dream up could be made in this lab that doubled as a machine shop.

My eyes panned from side to side as I took in the sights and sounds. I ducked as a drone dive bombed us. It buzzed over-head, circled the room, then landed at a table by Ian.

He chuckled, amused.

Ian had curly white hair and a white beard. I guessed he was in his late 50s. He reminded me of Santa Claus curly hair, rosy cheeks, and a reddish nose. He wore a white lab coat and a white shirt and pants underneath. He had a round belly and looked like a jolly fellow. He wore small wire-rimmed glasses and looked pleased to see us. "What took you so long?"

"I told you I'd be by when I could," JD said.

"Did you not understand the urgent nature of this meeting from my dire tone?"

"Ian, you said to drop by at my convenience. There was nothing urgent about it."

"Well, you should have known what I was thinking," he said sharply.

JD glanced at me like he regretted coming to the Institute. "Oh, I'm a mind reader now? You'd get along great with my ex-wife."

Ian frowned at him. "This is no laughing matter."

JD raised his hands innocently. "Okay, okay. What did you want to see me about?"

He leaned in and whispered, "I'll tell you in a minute." He nodded to a coworker that was nearby.

Apparently, Ian wanted privacy.

Ian momentarily changed the subject. "Have you seen our latest developments?"

He pointed to the dive bomber. "This is a stealth drone. Virtually undetectable. Makes no sound, has forward-looking infrared, night vision, and the ability to carry small payloads. It has several military applications. Remote-controlled and has a range of 17.2 miles."

He motioned for us to follow him through the lab.

Ian led us to a small ROV that sat atop a table. It was yellow with black accents. *Explorer 2* was written across the side. It was 10 inches wide and 14 inches long. It had two articulated arms for grabbing specimens and manipulating objects.

"This is my latest ROV. Capable of depths up to 6000 meters and beyond. The beauty of it is the acoustic communication module. It allows for wireless control underwater. It has a pulse based modulation scheme which uses a demodulation algorithm and dynamic—"

"In English," JD said.

"It can be controlled wirelessly up to 1.7 kilometers. The military is interested in these for placing and diffusing mines. It weighs 12.2 kg, has a forward speed of 4 kn, and can lift up to 30 pounds." Ian had a proud smile on his face. "Want to try it out? I've got one in the tank you can fiddle around with."

It looked interesting, but I wasn't in the mood to fiddle around. "Maybe later."

He waved us on to the next item that he wanted to show us. "This is the ADS 9000. An atmospheric diving suit that's capable of depths up to 12,000m. This is a game changer.

Made from a special composite alloy, also my design. This will change deep sea rescue and repair operations."

The diving suit looked like a big, yellow, hard shell version of an astronaut's extra vehicular activity suit.

Ian continued boasting. "The suit has a state-of-the-art rebreather, onboard propulsion system, temperature control, and vital signs monitoring. You could walk around the bottom of the ocean for two days with this suit. Of course, it might get a little uncomfortable."

It was impressive technology, no doubt.

He led us to a companion yellow submarine that sat perched in the bay not far from the atmospheric diving suit. It was a three person submersible the size of a moving truck. It sort of reminded me of a bumblebee—big and round with long articulated arms, and lots of lights that looked like bug eyes.

"The *Trident* is made of the same composite material as the ADS. It has an airlock which is capable of launching the diving suit. It has advanced O2 scrubbers, climate controls, and all the modern conveniences. What do you think?"

"Impressive," I said. "And you designed all of this."

"That's why I get paid the big bucks."

"This is all great, Ian, but I know you didn't get us over here just to give us a tour," JD said.

Ian glanced around to make sure his coworker wasn't in earshot. Then he whispered, "I have a situation."

He let it hang there a moment for dramatic effect.

"It's a very delicate matter."

"Were you abducted by aliens and touched inappropriately?" JD snarked.

Ian scowled at him. "One of these days, Donovan, it's all gonna come out. You'll see. Our government has known about extraterrestrials for years—"

"Why are we here, Ian?" JD groaned, cutting him off.

Ian's face crinkled again. He didn't like being cut off, and he was avoiding saying what was on his mind. I could tell he felt embarrassed about it.

"I think my wife is fooling around," he finally blurted.

"Welcome to the club, Ian," JD said.

"I'm serious!" he said, with a scowl.

"What makes you think she's fooling around?" JD asked.

"Well... She started going to the gym." He said it like that, in and of itself, was proof. "She's lost weight. She's going out more with her *friends*," he said in air quotes.

"Do you smell cologne on her when she comes home?" JD asked.

Ian thought about it. "No. I don't think so."

"Does she take a shower right after she's been out for the evening?"

He shrugged again.

"Has she stopped having sex with you?"

His face twisted again. "That's none of your business."

"Well, if she's doing any of those things, that might be an indication that something's wrong."

There was a long, grim pause.

JD continued, "Look, in my experience, if you think your wife is fooling around, she probably is."

That wasn't exactly what Ian wanted to hear. "Could you do some investigating? Stake her out. See if she's meeting up with someone."

JD rolled his eyes. "Are you sure that's what you want me to do?"

"I'm positive. It's eating me up inside."

"Have you asked her?"

"No. She wouldn't tell me the truth."

"I know Claire. This doesn't sound like Claire. How long have you two been together.?"

"30 years!"

"30 years *is* a long time," JD muttered.

Ian glared at him again.

"What about you? Are you fooling around?"

Ian's nose twisted, offended. "Absolutely not!"

"Are you positive?" JD pressed.

"I am loyal to a fault."

JD sighed. "I really don't want to do this."

"Why not?"

"Because, what if I find something? Then you're always going to remember me as the guy who gave you devastating news. We've been friends for way too long."

"Why would I get mad at you?" Ian asked. "Just give me some peace of mind."

JD grimaced. After a long moment of internal debate, he said, "Okay. Fine. But don't say I didn't warn you."

"Thank you. Was that so hard?"

JD shrugged. "Sort of."

"And keep this under wraps. I don't want this getting out." Ian paused for a long moment. "But if she *is* screwing around, I want proof. Pictures, emails, texts. Anything I can use in the divorce proceedings."

"Easy there, cowboy," JD cautioned. "Don't go putting the cart before the horse."

"I'm a planner. I like to be prepared." He motioned to all of his toys. "This job... It will make you crazy. I have to build redundant systems into everything I design. I have to antici-pate every conceivable failure, every possible glitch. It's maddening."

"I can see that," JD said. "Maybe you should take a vacation?"

Ian sighed. "What's the point of a vacation? No matter where I go, I can't ever seem to escape from myself."

Ian thanked JD once again, and we said our goodbyes.

It was time for happy hour.

We hopped in JD's Porsche and drove to Oyster Avenue. It

was still early evening, and we were able to find decent parking a block over.

Oyster Avenue was a popular nightspot, lined with bars and restaurants. It didn't matter what night of the week, there was always a crowd. The week days were slower than the weekends, but you could always find good entertainment in Coconut Key.

Music echoed down the street from various live bands. A thin crowd of tourists strolled the sidewalks. The smell of grilled food and spices filled the air.

As we walked toward the entrance of *Riptide* I saw something I didn't expect. My stomach tightened, and I grimaced. I knew something was funky, and I kicked myself for not acting sooner.

14

The neon signage of *Forbidden Fruit* glowed as dusk fell over Coconut Key. Located across the street from *Riptide*, I had a clear view of the strip club's main entrance. The adult establishment was renowned for its fine selection of exotic beauties that could be seen in various states of undress. It would not be unusual to find celebrities or politicians inside, ogling the attractions.

Neither JD nor I were immune to the club's charms, but it was disconcerting to see Ryan, my sister's boyfriend, entering the establishment.

I pointed him out to JD as he stepped through the main doors.

JD shrugged. "So?"

"That's my sister's boyfriend!"

"So?"

"He's going into a strip club!"

"So?"

My eyes narrowed at him in frustration. "I don't think Madison would think too highly of that."

"When did you get so uptight?"

"I'm not uptight," I protested, clenching my fists. "I just don't want to see my sister get hurt."

"It's harmless fun. It's a proven fact that when men view naked women, their stress levels and blood pressure decreases. It's healthy. It reduces your risk of stroke and heart attack. Besides, he can work up his appetite, then go bang the snot out of your sister."

I glared at him. "You're not making me feel better about this."

"She's a big girl. She can take care of herself."

I sighed. "You're right. It's none of my business. She'll find out sooner or later if he's fooling around on her."

"It's happy hour at Forbidden Fruit. If you *really* want to, we could go in and spy on him," he said, trying to act ambivalent about it.

I could tell he really wanted to go. "Maybe one drink."

We darted across the street, weaving in between passing cars, and strolled into the den of debauchery.

A quick flash of our badges got us in without paying a cover. Spotlights slashed the foggy air, and smoldering beauties performed acrobatic maneuvers around chrome poles. Pop music pumped through large speakers, and a DJ introduced girls on each of the main stages.

I scanned the club, looking for Ryan. He was seated next to the main stage.

JD and I moved toward the back, trying to remain inconspicuous.

We had barely sat down when a waitress in fishnet stockings and black lacy underwear took our order. Even at happy hour, the drink prices were exorbitant. But you weren't paying for the liquor, you were paying for the view.

The view was pretty damn good.

I watched as Ryan stuffed a few dollar bills into a girl's G-string on stage. She tantalized him with her wares and gave him a kiss on the cheek. As far as value was concerned, it was probably the best bang for the buck in this club. But I was well aware that just about anything could be had for a price.

"What do you think? Should I tell Madison?"

JD's face soured. "What the hell is wrong with you? Snitches get stitches."

"Yeah, but she needs to know the kind of guy she's dating."

"Like you've never put a dollar in a girl's G-string?"

"That's different," I said, realizing my own hypocrisy. "I certainly don't want my sister dating guys like me."

"I think you're overreacting. What's the harm in helping a girl pay her tuition? This is a legitimate form of employment for women without higher degrees. It's a legitimate form of employment for women *with* higher degrees. Hell, do you know how much money some of these girls can bring home a night? Without sucking dick!"

I frowned at him.

"As long as he stays out here and doesn't go back into the VIP room to get a tug, it's not cheating," JD said.

I took a deep breath. "Okay. Fine. You're probably right. It's just harmless fun."

The waitress returned with her drinks, and JD started a tab. Moments later, two beauties fell into our laps, asking if we wanted company.

"My friend is a little tense," JD said. "I think he could use a little relaxation."

The brunette sitting in my lap sparkled "I'm an expert at relaxation techniques."

Before I could protest, the dancer unsnapped her bra with her svelte fingers. The French manicured nails looked almost luminescent in the dim club. The frilly fabric went slack, and two glorious mounds bounced free.

My eyes widened, taking in their round form.

She pushed them in my face and teased me. "I bet your troubles are melting away already," she said in a breathy, seductive voice.

I had to admit, she had achieved in distracting me, her toned body sliding against mine. She spun around and presented her assets. With the smack of her palm, she let me know just how toned she was. The red handprint on her ass cheek lingered, along with my eyes.

I was so temporarily smitten that I didn't notice Ryan had left his seat.

I peeled my eyes away from the brunette's body and glanced around the club to see Ryan disappear into the VIP area with a bottle blonde. The bouncer pulled back the velvet rope, and the two slinked down an alley to one of the private rooms.

I knew what went on back there.

"How about we take this somewhere more private?" I suggested.

The brunette's eyes brightened. "Oooh, I like that idea."

She took my hand and pulled me from the seat, leading me back toward the velvet rope.

15

The VIP room looked like a cheap motel room in Vegas. There was a leather couch, a small stage with a shiny pole, and a full size bed—which was just a thick leather mat on top of a black riser.

It was probably a petri dish of bacteria.

The room cost $200 for 15 minutes—2 drinks and a helluva private show came with it.

Serenity was the brunette's stage name, and for 15 minutes she was an angel—or a devil.

Whatever I wanted.

According to the rules, I had to remain fully clothed.

Though, I knew some of the girls were more than willing to break the rules—for an added fee, of course.

Serenity's body writhed and undulated as she moved to the music. She pressed her body against mine and whispered naughty nothings into my ear. Her hot breath on my neck, and her supple curves, stoked my desire. But I didn't come back to the VIP room to get my rocks off.

That wouldn't happen, anyway.

With my clothes on, I'd be left, high and dry. That didn't sound like much fun.

I stopped Serenity mid show. "Actually, I just came back here to talk."

"You paid $200 to talk?"

I nodded.

"I'm a good conversationalist." She smiled.

"I want you to do me a favor. A guy came back here with one of your coworkers. Do you think you could find out what went on in the VIP room between them?"

Her eyes narrowed curiously. "What do you want to know? Is he your boyfriend?"

I raised a surprised eyebrow. "No. He's dating my sister."

"Gotcha."

"He came back here with the blonde," I said. "Red lace lingerie. Shoulder length hair. Had a Marilyn Monroe vibe."

"Cherry Bomb?"

"No. Not Cherry."

"It's gotta be Mercedes," Serenity said. "Yeah, I can ask her after she finishes up."

"Thank you. I appreciate it."

"No problem."

"Does she do extras?"

"For a price. Are you looking for extras?"

"No," I said.

"You don't look like the type who has to pay for it."

I grinned.

"I don't do extras. But you *did* paid for a show, are you sure you don't want me to finish?"

"If you want to," I said, trying to sound disinterested.

A sly grin curled on her full lips. "Oh, baby, I want to."

She finished her routine, and as anticipated she left me feeling like an unlucky teenager on prom night. Our 15 minutes were up, and a bouncer knocked on the door.

I pulled myself together and tried to arrange things. My cargo shorts were fitting a little too tight at the moment. I tried to think about baseball statistics instead of Serenity's curvaceous assets as I walked down the hallway.

I rejoined JD in the main area who now had two girls dancing for him.

"Did you have fun?" JD asked.

"I put it on your tab, so, yeah. It was well worth it."

He scowled at me playfully. "I don't want to know. I'll get the bill soon enough."

The song ended and the two girls put their bras back on.

One sat in JD's lap, while the other took a seat opposite me. She sipped on a drink JD had bought her.

The waitress brought me another whiskey on the rocks, and JD nuzzled with a striking redhead named Sonja.

I glanced around the club, looking for Ryan, but I didn't see him anywhere.

A few minutes later, Serenity sauntered toward me. She leaned over, hanging her wondrous orbs in my face and whispered in my ear, "Mercedes said nothing happened. A little grinding, heavy petting, but he didn't want to pay for a tug or a BJ."

"Thanks for the info."

"Anytime."

I watched her saunter away to find another customer.

"Don't cry, ladies, but I think it's time for me to go," JD said.

The girls whined and made pouty faces.

Sonja said, "Don't go, Daddy!"

"Alas, I think I have already exceeded my budget for the evening," JD said.

There were more frowns and sad faces.

The only thing they were upset about was the end of their revenue stream.

JD's eyes bulged, and he swallowed hard when he got the bill. He gave the waitress a wad of cash, and we said our goodbyes.

We exited the club and stood on the sidewalk. The sky was pitch black now, and the nightlife of Oyster Avenue was in full swing.

"That was some happy hour," JD said.

He pulled out his phone and began to scroll through his contact list. He dialed Helen's number. After a few rings, she answered JD's call.

Within a few moments, his plans were solidified. He hung up the phone with an expectant grin on his face. "You're on your own for the rest of the evening."

I glared at him, envious. Serenity had gotten me all worked up for nothing, and I had no current booty call.

To me, going to a strip club was like buying a car that you could never drive. Fun to look at, but sometimes you just needed to get into the driver seat and run through the gears.

"You want me to drop you off at the marina?" JD asked.

"No. I think I'll stroll Oyster Avenue and see what kind of trouble I can get into."

He gave me a salute and said, "Happy hunting, sir."

JD spun around and headed down the sidewalk at a brisk pace.

16

I had a slight buzz and a pocket full of testosterone. That was a recipe for poor life decisions. But epic mistakes make for good stories over drinks.

Life is about the adventure.

I strolled down the street, contemplating my options.

Bumper was a dance club with thumping music, trendy twenty-somethings, and lots of designer drugs. Not really my scene, but the clientele was undeniably striking.

Tsunami Jack's was a casual beach bar that was always good for reggae music. Live bands would crank out Bob Marley covers that were nearly indistinguishable from the real thing.

Reefers had the same vibe, but Scarlett worked there, and it didn't seem like the best place to hang out for multiple reasons.

I made my way down to *Keys*—an upscale piano bar. It had that old-school vibe with mahogany wood panels on the walls, crown molding, and a bar full of top shelf liquor. The wait staff wore formal attire, and a pianist tickled the keys in the most sublime of ways.

The crowd was elegant and sophisticated—and that precluded my entry. The doorman stopped me as I tried to enter. "Can't let you in like that."

He didn't approve of my T-shirt and cargo shorts. This was a coat and collared shirt type of place. Slacks, dress shoes, no sneakers.

I was about to pull out my badge and throw my weight around when a sultry voice said. "He's with me."

"Yes, of course, Ms. Varga."

The doorman pulled the door wide and motioned for me to enter.

I smiled at Luciana and waved her into the bar before me. Two bodyguards in suits followed her, but I cut them off, stepping in line with Luciana. "Thanks. It seems you certainly have pull around here."

"It's one of my favorite places. Good music. Strong drinks. Nice clientele."

"Except for me, of course."

She looked me up and down. "I've seen you look better."

I arched an eyebrow at her. But at least she was honest.

"You clean up well. But this..." she looked over my attire. "This is dreadful."

I shrugged. "I worked a charter earlier. I didn't expect to be out on the town."

The maitre d' gave me a dire look as I entered. He scurried off to the coat room and within a few moments, he returned with a suit jacket for me.

I looked ridiculous.

I felt like JD wearing a suit jacket with a T-shirt and cargo shorts.

Luciana laughed.

I modeled the jacket for her, pretending to be on a runway at fashion week in New York.

She laughed even harder.

"I think that makes the ensemble worse," she said.

I shrugged.

"If you are going to be seen with me, we have to do something about that outfit."

She snapped her fingers, and one of her bodyguards stepped to her, ready to take orders. She looked me up and down, then whispered in his ear. He scurried away after receiving his secret instructions.

"What was that about?" I asked.

"What are you drinking?"

"Whisky. Rocks."

She smiled. "A man after my own heart."

She leaned against the bar and placed an order. The bartender eagerly filled two glasses and pushed them across the counter.

Luciana and I clinked glasses, and I took a swig of the fine whiskey.

"I thought you were going to stop by my office and take a look at the project plans," Luciana said.

"Sorry. I got sidetracked."

"Well, my offer still stands."

"Good to know."

She took a sip of her whiskey. Her full lips left a deep red stain on the glass.

We shared a lingering stare.

"So, what brings you out this evening?" she asked.

"Just blowing off some steam."

"I love this little bar. It's cozy, elegant, and they have some wonderfully talented piano players and jazz singers. I find myself here more than I care to admit."

"Had I known, I would have stopped in more often."

We shared another pause that was thick with unspoken tension.

"Tell me, what did you do before you were a deputy for the Coconut County Sheriff's Department?"

I shrugged. "A little of this, a little of that."

"I see."

"And how long do you plan on volunteering for the department?"

"I don't know. I think it's just a temporary position. But, the job has some perks. I get a shiny badge, which gets me into a lot of venues. And, in some small way, I get to make the world a safer place."

"An idealist?"

I chuckled. "No. Just trying to do my part. You are either part of the solution, or part of the problem, right?"

"Amen."

We clinked glasses again.

I could watch that woman sip whiskey all evening. To say she had an alluring quality was an understatement. I was jealous of the glass.

"I can't imagine that a handsome man like yourself would find himself alone on a Saturday night. Surely you have options?"

"I'm not alone. I'm with you." I smiled.

Her eyes smoldered at me.

We ordered another drink and found a table. We sat and talked, listening to the piano player tickle the ivories. It wasn't long before Luciana's bodyguard returned with a new suit in a garment bag. He handed it to me.

"Try it on," Luciana said. "We've got to get you looking presentable."

"You want me to change right here?"

She arched a sculpted eyebrow at me. "If you like."

I smiled. "I'll find the restroom."

The men's room was elegantly appointed with fine Italian marble, floral arrangements, and an attendant with every imaginable fragrance of cologne. He took the garment bag and assisted me while I changed into the attire.

The *Alesci* suit fit perfectly. It was a complete ensemble with a spread collar shirt, slacks, and *Bandini* leather lace-ups. I admired the garment in the mirror.

It was a nice suit, and I knew it had cost over two grand.

I tipped the valet $20, stuffed my beach clothes in the bag, and returned to Luciana.

"Much better!" Her eyes sparkled.

"How did you know my size?"

"I have an eye for detail. And fashion." She smiled. "Do you like it?"

"I love it. What do I owe you?"

"For the suit? It's my gift."

I eyed her suspiciously. "You're not trying to bribe a deputy sheriff, are you?"

She burst into laughter. "If I was trying to bribe you, I would hand you a duffel bag full of cash."

I wondered how much cash?

"But, if it makes you feel better, perhaps we can arrange a trade?" There was a devilish tone in her voice, and her sultry eyes smoldered.

17

A fter a few hours, and a few more drinks, we were both pretty lit up.

Luciana may have been an evil real estate developer ready to kick Harlan out of his home. But she was also hot as hell, and I had to admit, we were having a good time.

The bar got pretty crowded as the night rolled on. Luciana suggested we find some place quieter. That some place happened to be her home.

Who was I to argue?

We piled into a large black SUV, along with her bodyguards and personal driver. We raced through the streets of Coconut Key in the black Cadillac Escalade that couldn't have been more than a month old. It still had that new car smell, and the scent of fresh leather filled the air.

Luciana put her hand on my thigh and eyed me lasciviously. Her hand traced its way up the *Alesci* inseam, and I did my best to pretend that I wasn't affected by her touch.

The driver kept eyeing me in the rearview mirror suspiciously.

Luciana liked playing games.

I was more than willing to be her sparring partner for the evening.

The SUV pulled into the circular drive, letting us out at the front door. Her home was nothing short of spectacular. A modern two-story right on the beach.

The entryway was tiled with imported Italian marble. The expansive living room had floor-to-ceiling windows that offered a picturesque view of the ocean. Though, I couldn't see anything but the pool through the windows. From the darkness, I could hear the waves on the beach crashing against the shore.

The house was built in a U shape around the pool, and the place felt like a resort.

The driver pulled the car around to the garage, the two security guards checked the area, sweeping the entire house. They returned to the living room and informed Luciana that everything was clear. She thanked them and dismissed them for the evening.

The two of them disappeared down a hallway, but I didn't imagine they'd be too far away in case of emergency.

"They're very protective of you," I said.

"I pay them very well to be that way."

"You must have a lot of enemies. Or you're extremely paranoid."

"A little paranoia is healthy, don't you think?"

I agreed.

"And, as you see, in my line of work sometimes people can get a little angry with me." She moved close and flung her arms around my neck.

We stared into each other's eyes for a long moment.

Then, she inched closer.

She planted her full lips against mine, and we melted into each other. Our tongues danced, and I could still taste the whiskey on her lips, and the cherry flavor of her lipstick.

Her hair smelled divine, and her skin was flawless.

My hands traced the curves of her waist and found their way down to her sweet cheeks.

I grabbed a handful, and a subtle moan escaped her lips. Warmth radiated from her body.

I pulled her tight against my body, and her leg wrapped around me. We swayed in the middle of the living room, entwined in a passionate embrace, trying not to fall over.

Still heady from the liquor, it was a challenge.

Soon her lipstick was all over my mouth, my cheeks, my ear, my neck. She ripped open the shirt she bought for me, and buttons scattered across the tile, rolling to hidden places under the leather couch.

The trail of lipstick made its way down my pecks, down to the abs that cost me 500 crunches a day. She unbuckled my belt, and before I knew it, she was making a fairly convincing argument that her project would indeed benefit the community.

Luciana excelled at oral arguments.

Before I was able to make a counterpoint, she slinked out of her dress and pulled me onto the leather couch.

Our naked bodies collided.

We did our best to break the mid-century modern furniture, but it survived our pummeling.

Moans of ecstasy filtered through the cavernous house.

I was so lost in the moment that I forgot all about the security guards. Surely they could hear? At that point, I didn't care who heard.

When it was all said and done, we collapsed on the couch, sweaty and breathless.

I buzzed with euphoria—and a little guilt.

What was I going to say to Harlan?

I may have been sleeping with the enemy, but I was sure he would understand.

Whatever momentary guilt I felt quickly vanished. I basked in the afterglow for a few moments, staring at the ceiling with Luciana in my arms.

Her delicate fingers stroked my chest. "Thank you. That was fun. I needed that."

"Thank *you*," I said.

"Maybe we can do it again sometime," she proposed. Then,

without missing a beat, "Javier will take you back to your home. Or to wherever you want to go."

I looked at her with a curious glance, a little shocked. "Are you kicking me out?"

She patted my chest. "You're a big boy. You can take it."

"Wham bam, thank you, man!" I said.

She mocked me, playfully making a pouty face. "Aw, are you feeling vulnerable? Used?"

I made a pathetic face.

She laughed. "Please. Don't even pretend to be upset. You just got to bang a hottie with no strings attached, and you didn't have to work at it."

"I worked a little."

She rolled her eyes.

"You bought me a suit, and in exchange, we had sex. Does that make me a gigolo?"

"I bought you a suit. We had sex. Two unrelated events." A naughty grin curled on her lips. "But, call it what you want, sweetie."

She pried her sweaty body off the couch and stood up. She bent over and scooped her dress from the floor. "Now, if you'll excuse me, I'm going to go take a shower and go to bed. I'll see you around, Deputy."

She vanished up the staircase.

I lay there for another moment, then got dressed. My shirt

hung open from the lack of buttons, and I definitely looked like I had a good time.

Her driver, Javier, waited for me by the car. He got the door for me, and I climbed into the backseat. He hustled around the front and sat in the driver's seat. "Where to?"

"*Diver Down.*"

As soon as the words escaped my lips, he dropped the car in gear and zipped out of the driveway.

In a few moments, we pulled into the parking lot of *Diver Down*. It was still open.

I thanked Javier, dug into my pocket for a tip, and handed it to him. He gave a nod of appreciation, and I climbed out of the SUV.

The Escalade sped away, and I stared at the restaurant for a moment. I decided I probably shouldn't walk into the bar looking the way I did.

I didn't know what I was going to say to Madison about Ryan, and I sure as hell didn't want to bring anything up tonight.

I knew there was a possibility that he was sitting at the bar, waiting for her to close down. I was usually pretty good about hiding my emotions—I had to be. You can't give yourself away when you're a clandestine operative undercover in a foreign territory.

But this was a little different.

I wasn't sure that I could keep my anger from showing through, which would most likely cause a scene.

I'm not sure why it got under my skin so much, but Madison was the only family I had left. I wanted to make sure she would be with someone who would treat her right.

I staggered down the dock and climbed aboard the *Wild Tide*. From the fridge, I grabbed a bottle of water and guzzled it down. I didn't want to be dehydrated in the morning—though I'd probably have to make a trip to the head in the middle of the night.

I descended the starboard stairs to the master suite, peeled off my clothes, took a shower, then climbed into bed.

I was out like a light, and the morning came way too soon.

JD pounded on the hatch, rattling the bulkheads. I peeled a crusted eye open as he poked his head into the cabin.

My temples throbbed, and my mouth felt like I'd swallowed paste.

"Rise and shine," JD trumpeted with an annoying grin.

I gave him a sideways glance.

He reveled in annoying me.

"What happened to you? You look like you got hit by a train!"

"I feel like I got hit by train."

"Obviously you found some trouble to get into last night?"

"Remember the developer?"

JD's eyes widened. "No way!"

"Yes, way."

"Impressive."

"She kicked me out afterward. I felt so violated," I said with a trace of sarcasm.

JD laughed. "Come on, get your shit together. We have to get up to Miami and talk to Nick Phelps."

It had completely slipped my mind.

18

Τhe howl of JD's Porsche as we blasted down the highway was like music to my ears. Top down, wind in my hair, music pumping, sun on my face —it didn't feel like work at all.

We were about halfway when my phone buzzed. Denise called telling me that, "The ballistics of Parker's gun doesn't match."

"Good to know," I said.

"I can say, definitively, that Glenn Parker was not shot with his own pistol."

"Thank you, I appreciate the call."

"Anytime."

"You think you can do me a small favor?"

"Anything." There was a little something extra in her voice.

"Can you run a background check on Ryan Johnson? Caucasian, 28, 6'1."

JD gave me the side-eye.

"Sure thing. Is he a suspect?"

"No. Personal matter."

"I'll call you as soon as I find something out," she said.

I hung up and slid the phone back into my pocket.

"You don't want to get into the middle of this," JD said. "All you're going to do is get Madison pissed off at you. People shoot the messenger, remember?"

"I'm not gonna be a messenger. This is just for my own satisfaction. I want to know what kind of guy she's getting involved with, that's all."

JD just shook his head.

We reached Miami considerably faster than I had anticipated. JD had a pretty heavy foot, and I don't think the Porsche went much under 100MPH at any time.

The registered address for Nick Phelps was the *Montana Heights* building on Brickell Bay Drive. It was a high-rise condo that offered stunning ocean views.

JD pulled into the drive and tossed the keys to the valet. He flashed his badge, and they parked the car in a spot near the entrance instead of driving it to a garage or side street.

We strolled into the main lobby. JD flashed a smile at the concierge as we made our way to the elevator banks.

A leggy blonde in a skimpy white dress stepped off the elevator with a small poodle on a leash. It tried desperately to keep up with her long legs and stiletto heels. The woman wore oversized sunglasses and had exquisite bone structure.

JD and I stepped onto the elevator after she exited, and her Chanel perfume lingered in the air.

"I like this building already," JD said.

We took the elevator up to the 36th floor and turned right down the hallway to apartment #3615.

JD rapped on the door several times, but there was no answer.

We waited a few moments, then knocked again.

Still nothing.

JD shrugged." Now what?"

"It's Sunday afternoon, and Phelps *does* own a boat. It's docked at the *Indigo Bay Marina*," I said, checking my notes on my phone.

It happened to be the same marina where Rory Tillman docked his boat. I didn't mention that fact to JD just yet.

A short drive later, and we were strolling down the dock toward Nick Phelps's boat, but it wasn't in the slip.

It didn't take exceptional powers of deduction to determine that Nick was most likely on the water.

"I guess we stay here and stake the place out until he returns?" JD said.

I nodded. "Why don't you hang tight. I've got some business to take care of."

"Business?"

"The guy who purchased my parents boat from Kingston. Rory Tillman. His boat is docked here."

JD raised his eyebrows. "Well, shit. Let's go talk to him."

We strolled through the marina, looking for the *Beeracuda*— it had been renamed.

When my eyes caught sight of the vessel, a chill ran down my spine, and a knot twisted my stomach. I swallowed hard with a lump in my throat, and my eyes brimmed. The boat looked exactly the same as I remembered. It had a new name and a few upgrades, but it was my parents' boat. There was no doubt about it.

My hands trembled slightly, and a thin mist of sweat formed in the small of my back. My cheeks felt flush.

"Are you okay?" JD asked.

"Yeah," I said, barely choking out the word. I took a deep breath. "Let's do this."

We marched to the transom, and I called into the salon. I could hear somebody fumbling around inside. A few moments later a man pushed through the hatch and stepped into the cockpit. It was Rory Tillman, I assumed. A quizzical look twisted on his face. "Can I help you?"

JD and I flashed our badges.

"I'm Deputy Wild, this is Deputy Donovan. Coconut County Sheriff's Department. We'd like to ask you a few questions about your boat."

"Is something wrong?"

"No. Nothing like that. You're not in any trouble. I just want to talk to you about your acquisition of the vessel."

He surveyed the two of us and hesitated a moment. "I bought it down in Coconut Key from Scott Kingston."

"Yes, I'm aware."

"Actually, I've been meaning to talk to him. I'm thinking about upgrading to a new boat, and he always did have sweet deals."

"Kingston is dead," I said.

That hung in the air for a moment.

Tillman looked astonished. "What happened?"

"He was murdered."

Tillman grimaced. "I'm sorry to hear that." He paused a moment. "What does all this have to do with me?"

"Did he ever mention anything about the previous owner of this boat?" I asked.

"Not that I remember. He said it was a single owner, well maintained. He had all the records and maintenance history."

They were likely all forged documents, I thought.

"Have you noticed anything unusual about the boat? Did you find any evidence of prior damage?"

His eyes narrowed curiously. "Now that you mention it, I did find a couple places that... well... that unsettled me. But I wasn't sure what to make of it."

JD and I exchanged a glance.

"Don't tell me this boat was stolen?" Tillman said.

I nodded.

Tillman frowned. "Come aboard. I think I've got something you might be interested in seeing."

19

J D stayed on the dock to keep an eye out for Phelps.

I scaled the transom of the *Beeracuda* and stepped into the salon with Tillman.

"I noticed a few places that looked like they had been repaired," Tillman said. "They'd done a pretty good job, but there had clearly been some damage to the hull. I pulled this out of a bulkhead."

He reached into a drawer in the galley and pulled out a twisted bullet that he had fished out of the fiberglass. He handed it to me.

My blood boiled.

I was holding in my hand a bullet that could have killed either of my parents.

At least I had something to go on. I could take the bullet back to the crime lab where it could be analyzed and cross-referenced against the database. Maybe it would match something, maybe it wouldn't? But I felt like I was one step closer to finding out who had murdered my parents.

"Thanks," I said. "This is helpful. You mind if I hang on to this."

"Keep it. It's yours," Tillman said. "Do you mind telling me what happened here?"

"I don't think you want to know."

Rory thought about it for a moment. "You're right. I probably don't."

"If you find any more items like this, let me know."

I wrote my number down on a piece of paper for him, thanked him for his time, and rejoined JD on the dock.

I turned back to Tillman. "You don't happen to know Nick Phelps, do you?"

Tillman rolled his eyes. "He's out here every Saturday and Sunday."

"I take it you don't think much of him?"

"He's an abrasive personality. Let's just keep it at that."

I thanked him again, and JD and I strolled down the dock. About an hour later, Phelps pulled into the marina.

We approached as he tied off the lines.

"Mr. Phelps," I said, holding my badge in the air. "I'm Deputy Wild, this is Deputy Donovan. Coconut County Sheriff's Department. We'd like to have a word with you."

A sour look twisted on his face. "I've got nothing to say to you."

JD and I exchanged a glance.

"Besides, aren't you two a little out of your jurisdiction?"

"We just want to talk to you about Glenn Parker."

His sour look turned even more so. "I don't have anything nice to say about that guy."

"When was the last time you were in Coconut Key?" I asked.

His gaze turned curious. "Why?"

"Parker's dead."

He chuckled. "Good."

"When was the last time you saw Parker?"

"Like I said, I don't have anything to say to you. Talk to my attorney."

Theoretically, that's where our line of questioning had to end. I gritted my teeth, and JD frowned.

"We can do this the easy way, or we can do this the hard way," I said. "We can come back with a warrant."

"Good luck with that. On what grounds?"

At this point we didn't have any probable cause.

"I know my rights," Phelps barked. "And you two can go fuck yourselves!"

Phelps locked up the cabin, stepped off the boat, and strolled away down the dock.

JD leaned in and muttered to me. "Son-of-a-bitch doesn't know his rights. That boat is on the water, and the Coast Guard can board and search it any time without a warrant or without probable cause. Title 14, section 89 of the United States Code."

JD grinned, slid his phone from his pocket, and called a buddy of his in the Coast Guard. Within an hour, a patrol boat arrived. A chief petty officer stood on the deck and shouted to us on the dock. "Which one of you is Jack Donovan?"

Jack raised his hand and flashed his badge. "That would be me."

"Commander Braxton said you needed some assistance."

"Indeed. Would you mind boarding this vessel and taking a look around?"

"Why?"

"It belongs to a *person of interest* in a murder case."

That seemed to be reason enough.

The chief ordered two petty officers to board the vessel.

"What are we looking for?" a petty officer asked as he stepped into the cockpit of the *Fuelin Around.*

"Murder weapon. 9mm," I said.

The petty officers kicked open the hatch to the salon and began tossing the boat.

JD grinned with anticipation, rubbing his palms together. "I love this shit."

"How do you know Commander Braxton?" I asked.

"Old fishing buddy," JD said.

After a 15 minute search, a petty officer emerged from the salon and stepped into the cockpit dangling a 9mm from his gloved fingers. "This what you're looking for?"

"Could be," I said.

The Coast Guard officially took custody of the item, then transferred it to the Coconut County Sheriff's Department.

The second petty officer emerged from the salon with something a little more damning. "I'm guessing this isn't baking soda?"

He held up a brick of cocaine.

That was enough to put things in motion. The Coast Guard contacted Miami-Dade, and a warrant was issued for Nick Phelps's arrest. They also got a judge to sign off on a warrant to search his condo.

All in all, I'd say it was a productive afternoon.

JD and I coordinated with the local PD, and they allowed us to tag along when they served the warrant. The look on Phelps's face was priceless when the tactical team kicked in his door.

The tactical squad stormed into the condo, weapons drawn, shouting. It was pure chaos for a few moments until the area was secured.

Phelps was face down on the ground with several assault weapons pointed at him. An officer slapped cuffs around his wrists and yanked him to his feet.

"What the hell is this about?" Phelps growled.

"You're under arrest for possession of cocaine with intent to distribute," an officer said.

Phelps's face tensed, and he glared at JD and me.

It was hard not to grin as they dragged him away in cuffs.

"You have the right to remain silent..." an officer began.

"I want to speak with my attorney," Phelps demanded.

He was taken to the station, fingerprinted, and put in a holding cell until he could be transferred to the County Jail. Phelps was facing federal drug charges, and he wasn't about to talk to anyone.

Detective Murphy was in charge of the investigation and had some interesting information to share with us.

20

"I don't know if this helps you out," Detective Murphy said, "but we pulled credit card records as part of our warrant. It looks like he was in Coconut Key around the time your victim was murdered."

A thin smile tugged at my lips and I shared a glance with JD.

"Think he's your guy?" Detective Murphy asked.

I shrugged. "It's the best lead we've got so far."

"Let me know if I can be of any further assistance."

We shook hands with the detective and headed back toward Coconut Key. My stomach was rumbling, so we stopped to grab a bite to eat at a Cuban restaurant at the edge of town.

Jack ordered the chicken quesadillas, and I got the Alambre de Pollo—chicken with refried beans, guacamole, mushrooms, onions, and flour tortillas.

The meal was pretty damn good.

We had skipped lunch, and my stomach had become a sour pit of acid, churning for a meal. The chicken hit the spot.

The restaurant was a cool little joint, decorated in yellow and teal colors, with bright art on the walls. Latin music filtered through speakers in the ceiling. Close your eyes, and you could be in Havana.

Denise called just as I was finishing. "Looks like your guy, Ryan, is clean. Nothing major. A few unpaid parking tickets. A misdemeanor public intoxication. He's just your ordinary, average guy with a wife and two kids."

My jaw dropped.

I was speechless for a moment, then I pulled myself together. "Thanks! That's helpful."

"That's what I'm here for."

I hung up the phone and shared the information with JD.

His eyes bulged, and he changed his tune. "Okay. Maybe I was wrong. Maybe it's good that you investigated this guy."

A proud grin crawled on my lips. I folded my arms and leaned back in the chair. "See. Trust your gut."

"I still think you shouldn't get involved."

"I'm not getting involved."

"She'll hate you if you ruin this."

"I didn't ruin anything. Her boyfriend did."

JD raised his hands in surrender. "I'm just saying..."

I gave his advice consideration. He was probably right.

Madison would get mad at me for interfering in her affairs. She was a big girl, and she could make her own decisions.

I decided I would leave it up to her. She would find out the truth, eventually. I just hoped it would be before this relationship progressed into something serious. I didn't want to see her get hurt.

The amber rays of sunset blanketed the sky. We raced back to Coconut Key and stopped at the station to drop off the evidence. With any luck, the lab could match Phelps's gun to the slugs pulled from Parker's body. I had the lab analyze the bullet from the *Beeracuda* as well.

It was 11 PM by the time JD dropped me off at the marina. I didn't bother going into *Diver Down*. I figured I would see Ryan, and it would just piss me off.

I strolled down the dock to the *Wild Tide*.

Before I reached the boat, my phone buzzed. It was a text from Luciana. *[Are you busy?]*

[Not really.]

[I'm sending a car for you. I have needs.]

[Ok.]

I replied without hesitation. I figured I would let her use me again. There were worse things in life.

I turned around and strolled back down the dock to the parking lot. Within a few moments, the familiar black Cadillac SUV pulled beside me. I climbed into the backseat and slid into the supple leather seats.

Javier said nothing as I buckled my safety belt. He drove me to Luciana's house and didn't bother to get my door. I hopped out and strolled to the door and pushed into the entrance foyer.

"It's me, don't shoot," I said as I made my way into the living room, looking for the spicy brunette.

Sensual music filtered through the house.

"I'm upstairs," Luciana shouted. "Make yourself a drink and pour me one too."

Whiskey crackled over the ice cubes as I poured two glasses. I took a sip and eagerly headed up stairs. I followed the sound of her voice to her bedroom where she greeted me with a passionate kiss.

She was wearing a set of black lacy lingerie complete with a garter belt and stockings. She looked like something out of a Victoria's Secret commercial. Her delicate fingers took the glass of whiskey from my hand and she brought it to her full lips, once again leaving a luscious stain on the glass.

She spun around and sauntered toward the bed like she was walking a catwalk. She had a mesmerizing sway to her hips. She crawled onto the bed like a cat stalking its prey and purred. With a curled finger she beckoned me closer.

Who was I to say no?

I had seen hide nor hair of the bodyguards, but I knew they were around. They would never be far. For the time being, I was her bodyguard, and I did my best to protect every supple curve.

Once again, screams of ecstasy filtered through the house

with a passionate crescendo. I collapsed on top of her a sweaty, exhausted mess.

We lay together for a few moments, enjoying each other's delights. I figured she would kick me out momentarily, so I wanted to soak up the moment as much as possible. She was a passionate woman that burned with deep desire. She didn't do anything half-assed. Whether it was business, or romance, she was in it to win it.

I eventually rolled aside and caught my breath. I stared at the ceiling as she lay beside me. We didn't say anything. There was no need. This was strictly a business transaction. A mutually beneficial arrangement. Pure pleasure.

That's when I heard a dull snap downstairs. I recognized the sound instantly, and my eyes went wide.

It was followed by a thump and a dull groan.

I slid out of bed, pulled on my shorts, and drew my weapon.

Luciana sat up in bed, clutching the sheets across her breasts, her eyes wide as I padded to the door and held up behind the frame.

I heard another snap, followed by a thud, then a thump. A body had hit the wall and fell to the tile.

The term silencer is a misnomer. It's a suppressor. It attenuates the report of gunfire. But it doesn't make it silent. Not like you see in the movies.

Someone was downstairs and had just taken out the two bodyguards.

21

"Call 911," I whispered.

I pushed out of the bedroom and moved down the hall toward the stairs, keeping my weapon in the firing position, trying not to squeak the floorboards.

An assassin lurked somewhere below.

I waited at the top of the landing, looking down into the living room for movement in the shadows, reflections in the glass, etc.

The air was still and thick with tension.

I hovered a moment, waiting, listening. The constant click of a wall clock in a nearby room sounded thunderous in the silence.

Initially, I assumed there was a single assassin. But there could have been more.

There probably was.

It was standard protocol on high-end jobs. When you absolutely, positively, had to kill someone, why send just one killer?

I moved back down the hall to the bedroom and announced myself to Luciana with a whisper. "It's me."

I hovered in the doorway.

Luciana was still in bed, but she had pulled a pistol from a drawer in a nightstand by the bed.

"How many?" she whispered.

I shrugged.

The bedroom opened to a terrace that overlooked the water.

It was a big concern. I kept an eye down the hallway to the stairs and glanced to the terrace that lay beyond the sliding glass doors.

My heart beat elevated, and my temples pulsed. My hand gripped the pistol tight.

Footsteps on the roof creaked overhead. The tiny, muffled sound of asphalt granules breaking loose underfoot filtered down.

I pointed to the ceiling as I stepped into the bedroom. I quietly pulled the door closed and locked it. It wouldn't keep an intruder out for long, but it would slow them down.

I pointed to the door and whispered, "Shoot anyone that comes through."

Luciana nodded.

I crept across the bedroom toward the sliding glass doors, knowing someone was right above me on the roof.

My hand reached for the latch, and I unlocked the sliding glass door. It made a click that was way too loud.

I grimaced, angry with myself. I had given away my position. Whoever was on the roof knew exactly where I was.

Fuck it.

I slid the door open, making a ruckus, then backed away, keeping my weapon aimed at the terrace.

Sheer curtains blew in the breeze.

Suddenly, the bedroom door shattered, flying off its hinges as an assassin kicked it open.

BANG!

BANG!

Muzzle flash flickered from the barrel of Luciana's pistol.

My ears rang from the deafening report.

She drilled two bullets into the chest of a masked assassin as he stepped through the mangled doorway. Blood exploded from his chest, and he fell back to the ground. Gurgling gasps of breath escaped his lips as he drowned in his own blood and fluids.

At the same time, the other assassin dropped from the roof and opened fire.

Bullets snapped across the room from a suppressed pistol. They whizzed past my ear, and a gentle breeze tickled my skin.

I took aim and squeezed off two rounds, putting one into the attacker's chest, and the other into his face.

He crashed to the terrace, and blood pooled around his body. His weapon clattered against the tile. His body twitched for a few minutes with nerve impulses.

I moved to the thug in the doorway and kicked his weapon down the hall for good measure. But he wasn't getting up.

Neither was the guy on the terrace.

I pulled off the attackers' ski masks. They had gang tattoos on their faces and necks.

I grimaced.

Julio Ruiz was the head of a powerful Mexican cartel, but surely his people had realized by now that I didn't kill him? Cartwright did.

These clowns could have been locally hired assassins, but it seemed like a stretch. I don't think the Mexican cartel was behind this. There were numerous people who wanted me dead. Too many to count.

Sirens echoed in the distance.

Before long, the house was swarming with EMTs and a tactical response team dressed in black with assault weapons.

"What the hell happened here?" Sheriff Daniels asked, surveying the carnage.

He didn't look thrilled about being pulled out of bed this time of night. He was dressed in civilian clothes with a badge affixed to his shirt.

I stood in the bedroom, shirtless, while Luciana barely had time to find a red silk robe. A Komodo dragon print slithered around her taut form, and the hem rode high on her tanned thighs.

The sheriff's cranky eyes flicked from me to her, then back again. He didn't have to say anything to express his disapproval. His eyes said it all.

"I'm guessing these two men weren't here to steal the TV?" Daniels said.

"I've had some run-ins with the cartel in the past," I said.

"That doesn't surprise me," Daniels replied. He surveyed the bodies. "But these aren't cartel. See that tattoo?" he said, pointing. "These guys belong to *Los Sombríos Segadores*. Local gang. Street thugs. Low level dealing, extortion. That kind of thing. What did you do to piss them off?"

I shrugged. "It's my charming personality."

"That would do it," Daniels said, dryly.

The crime scene photographer snapped photos, we made statements, and Brenda examined the bodies.

Daniels pulled me aside, making a subtle nod to Luciana. "What the hell were you thinking?"

"What do you think I was thinking?"

"She's a major contributor to the mayor's campaign. A prominent social figure. This is not going to reflect well on the department. These men were here for you!"

"I have a large fan club, what can I say?"

The sheriff's eyes narrowed at me.

"We don't know they were here for me," I said, not quite believing it myself.

"I've got three dead bodies, including her driver," the sheriff grumbled. "I'm going to have a lot of explaining to do about how and why this happened. Hopefully the press doesn't get wind of this. They'll have a field day. And the mayor won't be pleased."

"What do you want me to do?"

He just shook his head and marched away. "Miss Varga, would you like me to post a unit outside for the rest of the evening?"

"I think, perhaps, that would be wise," she said.

The bodies were removed and hauled off to the medical examiner's office. The crowd cleared out, and the house had an eerie stillness about it after everyone left.

"Would you mind staying for the rest of the evening?" Luciana asked. "I don't want to be alone."

"Sure. No problem."

"Thank you," she said as she embraced me, clutching tight.

I wrapped my arms around her. The pounding of her heart thumped against my chest. "Are you sure you wouldn't feel more comfortable somewhere else?"

"I have an island retreat. I may go there tomorrow. But I'll be safe here with you, and the sheriff's deputies outside." She smiled.

"You're pretty handy with a pistol," I said.

"I think it's wise to be prepared. I go to the range at least once a week."

It was almost 4 o'clock in the morning, and neither one of us could sleep. Adrenaline still coursed through my veins.

"Do you want breakfast?" Luciana asked. "I don't think I can get to sleep."

I nodded.

We moved to the kitchen and Luciana scrambled eggs and fried bacon. She didn't strike me as the domestic type, but she was quite adept in the kitchen.

We sat at the breakfast table and ate, talking until the sun came up. Even with a cup of coffee, I found my eyes drooping after the adrenaline had worn off.

The doorbell rang, and I perked up instantly, drawing my weapon.

"It's okay," Luciana assured me. "I made a few phone calls and arranged for two more bodyguards."

"The last two didn't work out so well," I muttered.

"Fortunately, you were here. I don't think I would have made it through the night without you. Thank you."

I made my way through the living room to the entrance foyer. I peered around the corner and could see two men standing on the porch through the frosted glass.

I was pretty sure that assassins wouldn't ring the bell, but I was cautious nonetheless.

I shouted through the door, wondering where the other deputies were. "Who is it?"

"We are here for Miss Varga. Rodrigo sent us."

I glanced to Luciana, and she nodded with approval.

I pulled open the door and allowed the two men to enter. I looked to the street and the patrol car was gone. The deputies had left.

I shook my head and grumbled.

Luciana told the replacement guards what had happened, and they assured her that the situation wouldn't happen again.

I assumed they were from the same agency as the other bodyguards.

Luciana showed them around the premises and addressed concerns and weaknesses in the overall security. There was no forced entry. The assassins must have slipped in through an open window or an unlocked door.

Once Luciana had given the new bodyguards their instructions, she took my hand and pulled me back up to the bedroom. We both crashed hard, and when I woke at noon, she was gone.

There was a note beside me on the bed that read, "Thanks for keeping me safe."

She drew a smiley face on the note.

22

I bit my tongue when I walked in to *Diver Down* and saw Ryan at the bar. Didn't this guy have some place else to be? I mean, didn't his wife wonder where he was?

I took a seat at the opposite end of the bar and tried not to glare. Harlan was in his usual spot, and I didn't have the heart to tell him that I had made friends with the person trying to kick him out of his home.

Madison eventually strolled down and took my order. It was around noon, and by this time, I was hungry again. "I'll take a bowl of crawfish bisque."

"Where have you been?"

"I spent the evening with a friend."

"You look like hell!"

I forced a smile. "Thanks."

I didn't feel the need to tell her that someone had tried to kill me last night. I maintained a smile and waved back at Ryan who flashed his pearly whites at the end of the bar.

Denise called from the sheriff's office. "Ballistics came back on the weapon you confiscated from Nick Phelps."

"And?"

"Not a match."

My jaw dropped. "Really?"

"Really."

"I thought sure we'd get a hit on that." I sighed. "Anything on that bullet I gave to the lab?"

"They are still cross-referencing the database. I'll let you know if anything turns up."

"Thanks."

I ate my meal and contemplated the case. Just because Nick's weapon didn't match the slugs didn't mean Phelps was innocent. He could have tossed the 9mm, or it could be somewhere else? There were endless possibilities, and I was no closer to solving this thing.

I stormed back to the *Wild Tide*, took a shower, and put on a fresh change of clothes. As I was getting dressed, Sheriff Daniels called. "Get over to Dowling Street, ASAP!"

"What's going on?"

"You have to see for yourself. Bring numb-nuts with you."

I called JD. He swung by the marina to pick me up, then we headed to the crime scene.

It was probably the most horrific thing I'd seen in Coconut Key. We usually didn't have crimes that made this much of a statement.

A man had been murdered, and his body had been carved up into sections and scattered across the street. Flies buzzed around the bloody remains. Neighbors looked on in horror at the spectacle. The forensics photographer documented the gruesome scene, and the medical examiner tried to piece things together, no pun intended.

Dowling Street was a shady part of town. Drug dealers and prostitutes worked the area on a regular basis.

"From what I've been able to gather from the residents, that's Diego Ortiz, a low-level drug dealer with gang affiliation," Daniels said. He pointed to a severed arm, covered in tattoos. "Just happens to be the same gang affiliation of the men who tried to kill you last night. *Los Sombríos Segadores.*"

His eyes pierced into me.

"I had nothing to do with this," I said, raising my hands innocently.

The tattoo was a grim reaper skull with *LSS* in fancy script underneath it.

"I'm just wondering what the hell is going on here?" Daniels said.

"Any witnesses?" JD asked.

"Nobody's talking," Daniels said. "They're afraid of gang retaliation."

"Understandable," I said.

"I've notified the next of kin, but they didn't want to answer any questions either. You might have better luck."

Daniels gave the address of Diego's mother.

"See what you can find out," Daniels said. "But I don't have high hopes for this one."

JD and I left the scene and drove a few blocks to Diego's mother's house. It was a small, but well maintained, one-story with three bedrooms and a porch.

"They're not going to talk to us," JD muttered as we strolled toward the door. His red 911 looked out of place in this neighborhood.

JD pulled open the screen door, and I knocked.

A few moments later an older woman cracked the door. She had dark hair that was graying on the sides and dark eyes.

"Mrs. Ortiz?" I asked. "I'm Deputy Wild, this is Deputy Donovan. I'm so sorry for your loss. I know this is a difficult time, but any information you could give us would be helpful."

"I told you people, I don't want to talk to you. Go away."

"Ma'am, we understand your concern, but we really have nothing to go on."

"I have other children to think about. Now go away before someone sees you here."

She slammed the door in my face.

"Told you," JD said.

I thought for a moment. "Come on. I've got a plan."

23

We cruised through the neighborhood in Jack's Porsche, looking for street transactions. Since we weren't beat cops, and didn't work the area, we were unknown to the local dealers. Hell, we could probably just pull up to a corner and someone would approach us within moments.

We didn't have to look too hard. Within a few blocks, I spotted money changing hands, and a small bag of dope was passed inconspicuously from dealer to client.

JD screeched the Porsche to the curb, and I hopped out of the car with my badge in one hand and my pistol in the other. "Freeze. County Sheriff!"

Eyes went wide, and both the dealer and the client took off running in different directions.

I chased the dealer across the street and down an alleyway. He hopped the fence into someone's backyard with grace and ease. It wasn't the first time he'd done it. He was a seasoned professional at the game.

I followed after him and wasn't quite as graceful.

I ran across the yard, avoiding a plastic baby pool, and several children's toys that littered the yard. I caught the dealer as he was scaling another fence. I grabbed his ankle and yanked him down to the ground.

His back smacked against the ground, and air rushed from his lungs with a cough.

With the barrel of my pistol pointed at his face, he was hesitant to make any sudden moves.

He raised his hands slowly.

"On your stomach, put your hands behind your head."

He complied, and I slapped the cuffs on his wrists. I wasn't gentle about it, and he groaned as I did it. Those steel cuffs could be nasty when smacked against the bones of the wrist.

The homeowner stepped into the backyard with wide eyes. She looked terrified.

I held up my badge. "County Sheriff. Everything is under control here, ma'am. Go back inside."

It was like something straight out of a cop show.

"What the fuck you want, man? I didn't do nothing," the dealer protested.

"Right." I said, my voice dripping with sarcasm. "I bet you got enough merchandise in your pockets to go away for a long time."

"Search me. I ain't got shit."

"You swallow it?" I asked.

"Bitch, I ain't swallow shit."

"Where you're going, you will."

"I ain't goin' to prison. I didn't do nothing."

"I'm happy to take you down to the station and keep you there till it comes out the other end."

It was common practice for dealers to keep drugs in small balloons in their mouths and swallow them in case of emergency.

"Tell you what. I'll make you a deal. You tell me what I want to know, I'll cut you loose."

"Fuck you."

"You clearly haven't thought this through. When I drag you out of here, I'm going to make sure the whole neighborhood sees us. Everyone's going to assume that you talked to me, because you're going to get out right away with no charges. People will think you had to cut a deal. Snitches get stitches."

"That's exactly why I'm not talking to your ass."

"Okay. I guess you'd rather get cut up in the street?"

"I don't know nothing about that."

"Sure you do."

The dealer didn't say anything.

I noticed an ant pile not too far away. Red ants swarmed about the mound, and there was a long line across the patio to the carcass of a dead bird.

I dragged the dealer through the grass and shoved his face millimeters from the swarming insects.

"Man, what the fuck are you doing? You crazy!"

"Start talking."

"This is like, harassment, or something."

"You ran from an officer, fell into an ant pile. That's what I recall." I shoved his face even closer.

His eyes widened as the crawly things scampered around his nostrils and eyes.

"Alright. Alright. Just get me away from these mother fuckers!"

I yanked his face away from the mound, and he breathed a sigh of relief.

"Diego was a low-level dealer. Mostly street stuff. But the last couple weeks he started moving higher end product. Dealing in higher volume."

"Do you know who killed him?"

"I don't know. He must have pissed somebody off. Stepped on some toes. You know how it is."

"You fucking with me?"

"No, man. I'm telling you everything I know."

"What about his gang? *Los Sombríos Segadores.*"

"Bunch of punks."

"Whose toes was he stepping on?" I asked.

"I don't know."

"Don't lie to me. You know damn good and well whose toes he would have been stepping on."

He hesitated a moment. "I don't really know, and I don't want to know. But the cartels have been moving in here. I'm so low volume that nobody gives a shit about what I do. But you start moving kilos, you've got plenty of people that want a piece of that action."

"Which cartel?"

"I don't know. They didn't hand out business cards."

I decided I had gotten all the information out of him I was going to get. I unlatched the cuffs and let him go. He didn't waste any time getting the hell away from me.

Instead of hopping the fence, I walked to the gate and out to the street. I called JD and told him where I was. A moment later the red Porsche whipped around the corner.

I climbed into the passenger seat and JD laid down some rubber. I told him everything I had learned. It was disconcerting to think the cartels were getting more active in Coconut Key.

24

"We're just in time to catch happy hour at *Blowfish*," JD said.

I shook my head. "No. Somebody will spit in our food."

JD's face crinkled. "I'm on good terms with Lily now."

"Don't you mean Kaylee?"

"Her too. We worked everything out."

My eyes narrowed at him.

"They're not mad. In fact, the three of us got together one night."

I gave him a skeptical glance.

"For real. Ask them if you don't believe me."

I sighed. "You're buying."

"Of course."

Blowfish was an upscale sushi bar, where the fish was fresh, and the women even fresher. Leggy ladies with sheer stockings, stiletto heels, and tight black leotards that somehow looked like formal attire.

"Table for two?" the hostess asked as we stepped into the establishment.

JD nodded.

"Right this way, Mr. Donovan."

She sat us at a table in the back, and within a few moments, Kaylee appeared, ready to take our order. "Good evening, gentlemen."

"Tell him you're not mad," JD said.

"Why would I be mad? You have to care about somebody to be mad at them." She smiled, then glanced to me. "You, on the other hand. I'm mad at you."

I shrugged innocently. "Why me?"

"You never called me."

JD eyed me curiously.

"Did you two hook up?"

"No!"

Kaylee smacked my arm playfully with the menu. "You didn't have to tell him that. You could have let him stew in it for a little bit."

I shrugged.

"Just because we haven't, doesn't mean we won't," she said with a hopeful glint in her eye, trying to make JD jealous.

Jack tried to act casual. "You two can do whatever you want. It's fine by me."

She huffed and her eyes narrowed at him, disappointed at his apparent lack of concern.

"So, is the food safe, or do we need to go somewhere else?" JD asked.

"Are you afraid you might die from eating bad blowfish?" she said with a sinister glare.

JD frowned at her.

"Do you guys know what you want?"

"I can think of a few things," Jack said with a grin.

"Sorry, Jack. That ship has sailed." She smiled and put a hand on my shoulder. "I'm on to bigger fish."

He rolled his eyes.

"I'll take a Kirin Light," I said.

"The same," JD added.

"I'll have two orders of salmon sushi, an order of otoro, and a California roll," I said.

"Spicy tuna roll, edamame, unagi, and two otoro."

"Are you sure you don't want to try the blowfish?" Kaylee asked with that sinister glint again.

JD smiled. "Maybe later."

Kaylee took our menus and turned our order into the sushi chefs.

"She's trying to get a rise out of me, but it's not going to work," JD said. "You can hit it if you want to. It's not going to bother me."

"Sorry. I don't need to follow in your footsteps."

He laughed.

Kaylee returned a moment later with our beer.

I took a sip and leaned back in the booth. It had been a hell of a few days.

A flash of recognition washed across JD's face. "Well, I'll be a son of a bitch. You know, it's been bugging me for the last hour."

"What?"

"The gang tattoo."

"The reaper design. It's the same as the ones on the assassins that you described."

"Yeah, I know."

"Glenn Parker's partner... His deckhand, what the hell was his name? Carlos? He had that same damn tattoo."

"Are you sure?"

"Positive.

"You think all of this is connected?"

"Damn right I do."

"We should go back and have another chat with Carlos. We could get the Coast Guard to search the boat."

"That may not be a bad idea," JD said. "But I think we should apply some subtle tactics first."

"What do you have in mind?"

A sly grin curled on JD's lips. "You'll see."

We sipped our beers, and Kaylee returned with our food. As always, it was like someone had just pulled it from the ocean, carved it up, and served it.

Jack paid the tab when we were finished, and once again, Kaylee gave me her phone number on a napkin. She leaned in and whispered in my ear, "Use it this time. Or I might serve you bad blowfish."

I chuckled and slipped the number in my pocket, having no intention of ever using it.

JD said he had to pick something up from his house, so we stopped by. Scarlett was on the couch watching TV. Her eyes brightened when she saw me. She sprang off the couch, ran to me, and flung her arms around my neck.

"What, no hug for me?" JD asked, with a sad look on his face.

I could tell a sassy comment was about to come out of Scarlett's mouth, but she thought better of it. She gave JD a hug as well. "I see you all the time. I don't see Tyson that much."

JD's face crinkled. "You see him all the time too."

"He saved my ass on more than one occasion."

"I've been saving your ass since you were knee-high to a grasshopper."

Scarlett rolled her eyes again.

"You remember who paid your attorney's fees, don't you?"

"Thank you, Jack."

He muttered to me. "It's *Daddy* when she wants something. It's *Jack* when she has no use for me."

Scarlett huffed and plopped back down on the couch. "He's so dramatic."

"Are you staying out of trouble?" I asked.

"Yes. And I'm bored to tears."

"Good," JD said. "We like boring."

Jack disappeared into his bedroom.

I asked Scarlett how she was holding up. She put on a good exterior. But she had been through a lot, and her close friend, Sadie, had died.

"I have mandatory drug and alcohol counseling and meetings. They've got me picking up trash on the highway, wearing an orange vest like some kind of convict. And let me tell you, there are people way more fucked up than me at these meetings."

"Well, you did do a few *extreme* things," I said, putting it mildly.

"Please. I got busted with a little coke. It's not like I was sticking needles in my arm and jacking cars for money. In rehab, I met one kid that had a thousand dollar a day habit. He broke into his parents house, stole a bunch of jewelry and guns, and pawned them. His parents pressed charges.

He OD'd, and he was legally dead when they brought him back."

"You OD'd."

She scowled at me. "Not on purpose. Somebody gave me something. It's not even the same."

"Well, I'm glad you are getting things together."

"All I do is work and watch TV. I have no social life. I will have no social life for the next two years."

"Might be time to enroll in class. You could probably get a lot of credits knocked out over the next two years without all the distractions."

"You're totally starting to sound like Jack. Please don't start to sound like Jack."

I raised my hands in surrender. "Okay. I will say no more."

She smiled. "We can talk about other things."

I searched for a topic.

"Tell me more about Bree Taylor," she asked with bright eyes.

"There's not much to tell."

"I love her. She's just so gorgeous. I mean, *was* so gorgeous."

There was an uncomfortable pause as the memory of Bree came flooding back.

"Will you take me to see her new movie?"

I hesitated. "I don't know…"

"Please," she begged with sad eyes. "Jack won't let me out of the house alone, unless it's for work. You can be my chaperone."

"That didn't work out so well last time."

"It's just a movie. We're not going to New York, or anything."

"Maybe. Ask Jack."

JD returned a moment later with a small device, and a devious sparkle in his eyes.

25

W e headed over to the *Sea Point Marina*. At this
      time of night it was pretty dead. The moon cast
      a pale glow through the clouds, and the boats
gently rocked on the waves. We tried to be inconspicuous as
we strolled down the dock, looking for the *Moby Debt*.

"You know, this isn't exactly legal," I said.

Jack's face crinkled at me. "We're just intelligence gathering."

Jack glanced around the harbor like a kid about to steal
something from a store shelf. He scaled the transom of the
Moby Debt, activated the GPS tracking device, and affixed it
to a metal plate underneath the fighting chair. Then he
hopped back off the boat like nothing had happened.

As we turned and strolled back down the dock, Rick burst
through the hatch into the cockpit. He held a pistol in his
hand, but the tension in his face evaporated when he recognized us. "Oh, it's you. I thought I heard someone board the
boat?"

"We didn't think anyone was here," JD said. "Sorry, I should have knocked louder."

Rick saw me eye his weapon.

"I keep this for self-defense. This marina is pretty safe, but now and then a boat gets stolen or broken into."

"Looks like a Bosch-Haüer XPP 9mm," I said.

"It is," Rick replied. "You know your weapons."

"Tools of the trade."

"Want to see?" Rick asked.

"Sure."

He pressed the mag release button and, and the magazine dropped into his palm. He stuck it into a pocket, then he pulled the slide and ejected a cartridge. It bounced against the deck and rolled. With the weapon empty, and on safe, he handed me the grip.

I took the weapon from him and admired the craftsmanship.

JD and I shared a nervous glance as Rick knelt down and picked up the bullet rolling around on the teak deck. From where he was, he could probably see the tracking device, if he knew where to look.

I sniffed the barrel of the weapon. It didn't smell like it had been fired in the last few days.

I handed the pistol back to him. "That's a nice gun. Good balance."

"I like it," Rick said, holstering the weapon. "What brings you out this way?"

"How is your new deckhand working out?" I asked.

"Good. He's a hard worker. Shows up on time. I can't complain." He paused. "I mean, I do worry about his background. I know he's got a little bit of a criminal history but... everybody deserves a second chance." He paused again and surveyed us curiously. "Why? Is something wrong?"

I shrugged. "Do you know if he is still affiliated with the gangs?"

"I really don't know anything about that. I mean, once you're in, you can't really get out, can you?"

"It usually doesn't work out too well for those who try," JD said.

"There was a gang member killed earlier today," I said. "We thought maybe Carlos might have some insight."

"We've got tomorrow off, but we have another charter on Tuesday. We'll be casting off around 8 AM, if you want to come by before then to talk to him. I don't know if he'd say anything to you, but you're welcome to try."

"Don't say anything to him. He might get spooked and not show up for work on Tuesday," I said.

"I understand." Rick took a deep breath. "Making any headway on Glenn's case?"

"Not really."

Rick frowned. "Sorry to hear that. Listen, if there's anything I can do to help, just let me know."

"You carry insurance for the business, right?" JD asked.

Rick knew where this was going. "Yes. Glenn and I purchased several policies. The boat is insured. We have a general liability policy. Then we took out a life insurance policy on each other in case something happened. I see you boys have done your homework, and I know where you're going with this. I'm the direct beneficiary of the policy. It will pay off the boat and put a little money in my pocket. So, that makes me a suspect. I get it. But insurance is not going to pay out until any questions about the nature of Glenn's demise is settled. So I stand to gain nothing as long as this goes unsolved."

"We had to ask," JD said.

"I understand."

"Thanks for your time," I said.

We strolled back down the dock, and Rick returned to the salon.

"Think he knows we planted the device?" I asked.

"We'll see, won't we?"

"How long will that tracker work?"

"We should get a week out of that battery. Maybe two," JD said. "I can track his movements on my phone and get alerts. Might turn up something, or might turn up nothing. We'll see if he's hitting the regular dive sites and fishing spots, or if something else is going on."

"Wait! What?" I said, staring in disbelief at the glittering diamond engagement ring Madison flaunted on her finger.

My jaw dropped, and I stared at the rock in a stupor as I leaned against the bar. JD and I had decided to stop into *Diver Down* for one last drink.

He was just as shocked as I was.

Madison beamed with joy.

She was positively glowing—rosy cheeks and radiant skin. "Ryan asked me to marry him!"

It came out as a high-pitched squeal.

"I gathered," I said in monotone. "How long have you known this guy? Two, maybe three, weeks?"

Her smile turned into a scowl. "You are supposed to be happy for me."

"It's a little fast, don't you think?"

She shrugged, flippantly. "When you know, you know. We just clicked. What can I say?"

I tried not to explode. "What can you possibly know about this guy in three weeks?"

"Everything I need to," she said.

She pushed away from the counter and attended to another customer down the bar.

"We need to have a little discussion. There are a few things I need to tell you."

Madison ignored me.

I exchanged a glance with JD.

He shook his head. "She's not going to shoot the messenger. She's going to blow the messenger up with an atomic bomb."

I frowned at him.

I re-fixed my gaze on Madison. "Can I have a word with you?"

"Say what you gotta say." She pulled the lever on the tap and filled a glass with beer. It foamed to a frothy head as she tilted the cup. She spun around and slid it across the bar to a patron.

"I think we should discuss this in private," I said.

She took the customer's money, made change, and slapped it on the counter.

He left her a few dollars for a tip which she promptly scooped up and stuffed in a glass jar at the register.

Then she decided to address me again. "So, you disapprove of Ryan? Big deal. It's my life. I'll do what I want. He makes me happy."

I couldn't hold my tongue any longer. "Did he tell you he's married?"

Her eyes narrowed at me.

"Did he tell you he's got two kids?"

"I told you not to do a background check on him."

"It's a good thing I did."

Her head shifted to the side, a sure sign of my impending demise.

Her jaw protruded as she scowled, preparing to unleash the heavy artillery. "He's in the process of getting a divorce. Yes, he told me about his wife and children! He's been transparent with me from the beginning. He's been separated for six months. Living on his own. It's just taking a while to go through the court system."

I shrank, feeling stupid.

"As soon as his divorce gets finalized, we'll start planning the wedding. But we both decided that we should wait at least a year to get to know each other better. But he felt it was important that he show me how much he is committed to this relationship by giving me a ring."

JD tried to hide his *I told you so* grin, but he failed miserably.

I had to eat a little crow. "I'm happy that you're happy."

Her eyes burned into me like lasers. "You know, I was just doing fine here until you came back into my life. Feel free to leave at any time if you're going to keep acting like this. We're not in high school anymore. You don't have to look out for me. I'm a big girl," she growled.

"You're right," I said raising my hands. "I overstepped my bounds. I'll stop acting like a big brother."

"Good."

She spun around and went back to her business.

JD gloated.

"Don't say a word," I cautioned him.

He finished his drink and stood up from the bar stool. JD patted me on the shoulder. He took a breath, about to say something, then thought better of it. "I'll talk to you tomorrow. I'll let you know if that tracking device registers anything interesting."

"Are you going to Helen's?"

"Yup."

He left the bar, and I decided to stroll back to the *Wild Tide*. My presence was no longer welcome in *Diver Down*.

I texted Luciana: [Just checking on you. Are you okay?]

I hadn't heard from her all day, which wasn't unusual. But given the fact that an assassination attempt was made on our lives, I thought I should at least touch base with her.

I stared at my phone for a few moments, waiting for a reply, but nothing came.

The marina was quiet, and the moon peeked through the clouds, glimmering across the water. I scaled the transom and pushed into the salon. I made my way down the starboard staircase to the master suite, kicked off my shoes, peeled off my clothes, and crawled into bed.

About the time I was dozing off, my phone dinged with another text message. It was from Luciana: *[Aw, you're sweet. I'm good. You?]*

I texted her back: [Want some company tonight?]

Again, I waited for a reply.

27

S orry, not tonight].

[The text from Luciana was short and succinct. There were no sad faced emoji's. No additional comment that would leave the door open for future contact.

Nothing.

I spent the next few minutes trying to analyze what exactly the three words meant. Did it mean she was tired? Did she have other plans? Was she just not in the mood? Or was she with somebody else?

I shrugged it off.

She didn't owe me an explanation, and I didn't need to be over-analyzing the situation. We hooked up twice and went through a traumatic event together. Perhaps it was making me feel a little closer to her than I should have been.

Tense situations can do that.

You will often find that couples that survive disasters

together end up connecting deeply and staying together for long periods of time. They share a common understanding of the trauma they experienced that no one else would ever understand. Hostage situations, survivors of airline disasters, carjackings. Anything that creates intense, heightened emotions can bond people, enhancing relationships and friendships.

Combat does it among platoon members. You'll never forget the buddies you went to war with. They are brothers for life. And most of them will do anything for you.

I tossed the phone aside and went to sleep—the gentle rocking of the boat aiding in my transition.

A shaft of morning light beamed through the porthole, and I peeled my eyes open, feeling rested. I yawned and stretched and checked the messages on my phone. Mrs. Parker had left a text message. *[Hey, it's Debbie. Do you still want Buddy?]*

I thought about it for a moment and tried to resist. What the hell was I going to do with a dog?

I couldn't hold out for long. I called her back right away. "Hey, it's Deputy Wild."

"You're in luck. My friend who took Buddy had a change of heart. Long story short, she had some unexpected expenses, and she didn't think she'd be able to care for him properly, especially at this stage. She started a second job... Anyway, I've got Buddy again. He needs a forever home."

I hesitated. "Sure. I'll take him."

"Great. I'll be here till noon if you want to swing by today. Or you can get him tomorrow."

"No, I'll come by today. Give me an hour."

"Sure thing."

I hung up the phone and lay back in bed, wondering what I just committed myself to?

I went over to Debbie's, and she greeted me at the door, holding Buddy in her arms. The other dogs barked and hopped around at her feet, and she tried to keep them at bay.

"His vaccinations are completed, but you'll have to take him in for a booster in a few months," she said.

Buddy looked at me with his adorable eyes. She handed him to me, and I cradled him in my arms.

"Is he housebroken?"

"He does pretty good. The other dogs have been showing him the ropes. So, he knows to go outside in the grass. Just let him go regularly and you shouldn't have any problems."

That was a relief.

Debbie petted him one last time, then asked Buddy, "You want to say goodbye to Mommy and Daddy?"

The dogs said their last words to each other, and Debbie looked like she was going to tear up.

The cab was waiting for me so I thanked her and took Buddy with me. I climbed into the backseat, buckled up, and held Buddy in my lap. He trembled slightly, not sure what was happening, or where he was going. I kept petting him, trying to reassure him that everything was going to be okay.

Back at the boat, I had his water bowl and food prepared. I had put newspapers on the deck in the guest room in case of an accident. I set Buddy on the deck in the salon and let him discover his new environment. He scurried around, sniffing and exploring.

I wasn't too sure how JD would feel about all this, but Buddy was hard not to love.

I played with Buddy for a while, then attached his leash and took him for a potty break.

"You want to go poop?" I asked.

Buddy tilted his head, curiously.

I figured I'd start training him to associate the word with the action.

I carried Buddy through the cockpit, scaled the transom, and set him on the dock.

Mr. Miller sat in the cockpit of his boat and gave us both a scowl.

I took Buddy around the back of *Diver Down*, by the dumpster, and let him do his business in the grass.

"Good boy!" I said.

I squatted down and gave him a treat and petted him, praising him with positive reinforcement.

I took him for a short walk, then we strolled back to the boat, and it was nap time.

I started crate training him right away. I let him explore the crate on his own, then gave him a chew toy while he was in there for reinforcement. In the evening, I took up his food and water bowl around 7 PM, that way he wouldn't overfill his bladder before bed. I put him in his crate before sleepy-time, and he whimpered a few times during the night, but I wasn't going to give into the demands of a Jack Russell Terrorist.

I set my alarm for an interval of 4 hours so I could walk him in the middle of the night and let him take care of business.

Over the next two days I spent as much time with Buddy as possible, looking after him, playing with him, and getting him acclimated to his new environment.

He seemed to be adjusting rather well, and there was no doubt I had grown fond of the little guy. Sure, it was a little extra work, but I liked having him around. He was a smart dog and picked up on things pretty quick.

I still hadn't heard anything back from Luciana, and I figured that it had pretty much run its course.

It was fun while it lasted.

JD called in the afternoon. "I'm noticing something interesting about Rick Lowden's boating activity. He's made several trips to the same location. All at night. I looked at the charts, and from what I can tell, there's nothing out there. No reefs, no shipwrecks, and it's not a particularly good fishing spot."

My brow crinkled. "What do you think he's doing out there?"

"I don't know. But I suggest we find out. You up for a little recon?"

28

I 'd been keeping clear of Madison for a few days. I figured she needed time to cool down. But I needed her assistance, and I felt reasonably confident that she wouldn't refuse. After all, Buddy could be mighty persuasive.

Buddy's paws clacked against the wooden dock as we strolled toward *Diver Down*. I hung onto his leash as he pulled me along. The little guy was full of energy, and I tried to get him out as often as possible, letting him run it off. Activity was always followed by a nap, for both of us.

I picked up Buddy and pushed into the bar and took a seat at the counter.

Buddy caught Madison's eye right away. He melted her heart, instantly.

She rushed over to greet him. "Who's this little guy?"

"Madison, meet Buddy. Buddy, meet Madison."

"He's so cute!"

She went gaga over him. Her fingers scratched his chin and petted his head. She took hold of him and held him in the air, and he licked her face.

"He's just adorable. Who's dog is this?"

"Mine."

She looked astonished. "Yours?"

I shrugged. "What? Is that so odd?"

"I never figured you for the nurturing type."

"Everybody needs a friend."

Her eyes narrowed at me. "You better be taking good care of him!"

"I am," I said. "But, I may need a little help."

She gave me a look, knowing something was coming.

"Do you think you could look after him for a few hours while JD and I go run an errand? I don't know how long I'll be gone, and I don't like to leave him for more than a couple of hours."

She hesitated for a moment. "I'm not adopting a dog by doing this, am I?"

"No."

"Are you sure about that? You're not just trying to pawn him off on me because you lack responsibility?"

"He's my dog, and I'm keeping him. Isn't that right, Buddy?"

Buddy barked in agreement.

"See."

"Okay. Fine," Madison said with a sigh.

"I'll bring down his food and water. Just make sure he gets out every couple of hours, and if I'm not back by 11 PM, put him in his crate for bed."

"Buddy, are you going to be okay with Madison?"

He barked again.

"You need to let him out in the middle of the night," I said. "So, set your alarm."

"I will." Madison didn't look thrilled about having her sleep disrupted.

"I'll bring down some treats and a few chew toys as well. You sure you don't mind?" I asked.

"I don't mind," she said, loving on Buddy.

I smiled. "You two are going to get along great!"

JD arrived, and we unhooked the lines and cast off. We idled out of the marina as the sun dipped down over the horizon. JD throttled up, bringing the boat on plane and we raced toward the mysterious destination.

It wasn't far from the dive site north of Angelfish Island where we had taken Ted and Charlotte.

"You don't think Rick is looking for treasure?" I asked.

A skeptical glance twisted on JD's face. "At night? And what are the odds he'd be looking for the Spanish Galleon in exactly the same place."

"It's not exactly the same place. It's at least a mile away."

JD shrugged. "We'll find out soon enough, won't we?"

We carved through the water, heading toward the site as the sky grew dark. JD flicked on the running lights, and by the time we arrived, the sky was a deep, midnight blue.

There was nothing out there.

JD cut the engines, and we drifted along the surface, rocking with the waves. I scanned the horizon, there was nothing but open ocean.

"Why don't you use some of that fancy equipment and tell me what's underneath the surface?"

JD glanced at the depth monitor. "We're 110 feet."

He took a look at the fishfinder.

JD had an *Aquasonic*™ HDX 6000. It had side-scan and down-scan imaging. It gave a complete view of fish, bait location, and bottom contours. It had a high-resolution display and provided information up to 700 feet on either side of the boat.

We made several passes of the area, scanning the depths below "I think something is down there," JD said.

"Like what? A shipwreck?"

"I don't know, but it's a man-made structure. Looks like it's about 75 feet long and 9 feet wide." He shrugged. "There is all kinds of shit at the bottom of the ocean. I've seen cars, trucks, cargo containers, you name it. Though, we're not in a direct shipping lane."

"I say we go down and take a look."

JD agreed.

We dropped anchor, prepped the gear, and prepared for a dive. JD raised the diver down flag.

We were both experienced divers and knew that we had a limited amount of bottom time at this depth.

We donned the gear and shouldered the tanks and plunged into the water. The beams of our dive lights lead the way as we descended through the dark depths. The underwater lights of the boat illuminated the surface area, but the light fell off fast.

At the bottom, it was black and inky.

JD and I stayed within sight of each other as we scanned the bottom with our dive lights. I saw a few fish and a crustacean scamper across the bottom, kicking up puffs of sediment. There was always the possibility of running into a bull shark or two, but as long as no one was chumming the water, I figured we'd be okay.

Including our descent time, we had a total of 15 minutes before we had to surface. On the way back up, we'd take a 3 to 5 minutes safety stop.

I had no intention of exceeding our bottom time.

Getting bent isn't fun.

My dive light cut through the darkness, slashing across the sea floor.

I didn't see anything.

Maybe what JD saw on the fishfinder was nothing more than a mound on the seafloor?

We were nearing the time when we needed to begin our ascent when my beam raked across a structure. I motioned to JD and pointed toward it.

As we swam closer, the object's full form came into view.

29

A black, homemade submersible lay at the bottom of the ocean, embedded into the sediment. It had been made in the swampy jungles of Columbia. Drug submarines were the latest weapon in the arsenal of the cartels for transporting large amounts of cocaine and heroin into the United States.

They were elusive and hard to detect.

There were three main designs that were in common use. This appeared to be one of the more sophisticated ones. I had heard of drug subs that had advanced sonar, air conditioning, heads, galleys, and sleeping quarters.

This looked to be an advanced model.

The typical crew complement was a captain, two deckhands, and an engineer. They were powered by diesel engines, and had ballast tanks, O_2 scrubbers, and even periscopes. There was no telling how many of these things were successfully navigating the waters. But many would-be sailors went to a watery grave at the bottom of Davy Jones Locker.

Sometimes the ships were scuttled to avoid capture, and the merchandise would be recovered later. Often, sailors drowned in the process.

I swam toward the main hatch. It had been opened from the inside, presumably as the crew attempted to escape—but a quick glance inside the submarine revealed none had survived.

The pale lifeless bodies of the crew floated in the sunken tomb. Fish had nibbled at their flesh and eyes.

The hatch wasn't wide enough for me to fit through with my gear on.

I looked at my dive watch—it indicated that we had less than 2 minutes remaining before we needed to begin our ascent.

We were cutting it close.

I slipped the tank off my shoulders, took a last breath from the regulator, then set the equipment on the seafloor. I swam through the hatch, into the tiny submersible. My dive light guided the way.

For something that was made deep in the jungle, it looked polished. No expense was spared. It was on par with a WWII era submarine. The only thing it lacked were torpedo tubes. And I wouldn't be surprised if that became an addition to later models.

I'm kidding, but not really.

I swam into the cargo hold and found it full of packages

sealed in watertight black plastic. They were stacked from the deck to the ceiling. Inside were sealed bricks of cocaine.

Several packages were missing, and I assumed that Rick had been making dives, attempting to bring the merchandise to the surface.

I couldn't quite put all the pieces together, but I gathered the two fishermen had stumbled across the wreckage and decided to make a few extra bucks. But something went wrong.

Two guys like Glenn and Rick wouldn't know how to move large volumes of cocaine. Perhaps that's where the gangs came in? They would need someone with street connections to move this volume of product.

With my knife, I cut open a package and grabbed a brick of cocaine. Upon examination, I saw it had the logo of the *Los Demonios Cartel* stamped into the packaging. It was a skull with devil horns.

I took the brick and swam toward the hatch. I squeezed through and showed JD the brick. He took the package and inspected it while I shouldered my tank.

JD pointed to the surface, indicating it was time we begin our ascent. We slowly made our way toward the surface and paused for a safety stop. The lights of the *Wild Tide* provided guidance in the dark inky water.

After the required safety stop, we surfaced and climbed aboard the swim platform. JD set the package of cocaine on the ledge and attempted to pull himself up. But we were greeted by barrels of angry assault rifles.

We had visitors aboard the *Wild Tide*, and they weren't

invited.

Another yacht had pulled alongside the *Wild Tide*, and men with assault rifles roamed the deck. It was a 90' Italian luxury yacht named the *Liquid Asset*.

The fact that the goons didn't put bullets in us right away was an encouraging sign. They allowed us to board the *Wild Tide* and remove our gear.

I recognized the thugs with machine guns—they were Luciana's replacement bodyguards. She emerged from the salon a moment later and was all business.

Rick was with her, and he looked terrified. His eyes were wide, and he fidgeted nervously.

My brow lifted with surprise.

If Luciana had any feelings about me one way or the other, she didn't show it. A goon took the brick of cocaine that we surfaced with and handed it to her.

"I see that you've found my submarine. I have to admit, I was hoping you wouldn't put this whole thing together, but you seem to be good at what you do."

I scowled at her complement.

"It seems we have a situation here," she said. "I have $250 million worth of cocaine sitting in that submarine. That is a considerable amount of product. I'm thankful that Rick and his former partner—what was his name—Craig?

"Glenn," Rick mumbled.

"...Right, Glenn. Fortunately they stumbled across it. I shudder to think that merchandise could have been lost forever. But those two dipshits decided to sell something that didn't belong to them."

Rick cringed as she glared at him.

Luciana held the brick of cocaine that was stamped with the cartel's signature mark. "Are you familiar with this brand?"

Every cartel marked their packaging with a distinct logo. It came in handy when recovering lost merchandise, or trying to find out who was moving stolen product.

"Any dealer on the street should have known who this merchandise belonged to," Luciana said. "Sadly, Rick and Glenn's entrepreneurial spirit was misguided. And they decided to partner with the wrong gang."

The *Los Demonios Cartel* had established a fearsome reputation for ruthless violence. I didn't know what level Luciana was in the organization, but apparently she was pretty high up.

Luciana smiled. "You see, those men who killed my guards the other night weren't there for you. They were coming after me. The *Los Sombríos Segadores* thought by taking me out of the picture, they could take my product with impunity."

"So you had Diego Ortez killed and carved into little pieces?" I asked.

"A demonstration. A warning to all who would dare cross me."

"An effective message," I said.

She handed the brick of cocaine back to one of her goons.

"So now what?" I asked.

"Now you work for me."

I arched an incredulous eyebrow. "Excuse me?"

"I need experienced divers to recover the cocaine from the sub. Rick can only do so much. Glenn became difficult and had to be taken care of. But now that I have you two, things should go much faster."

"You really think I'm going to help you?" I said, defiantly.

"I know you are."

I exchanged a wary glance with JD.

"I am aware of the difficulties of this task. The limited amount of time that can be spent at the bottom. The extended surface intervals. Believe me, I found out the hard way." She sighed. "I lost a good man."

"I'd be happy to contact the DEA," I said. "I'm sure they could help you get the cargo up very quickly."

She sneered at me. "I need all the merchandise on the surface within 48 hours."

I balked. "Impossible. Not unless you have a team of divers working around the clock."

"I'm growing impatient, and I'm tired of excuses. You're a smart cookie. Use your ingenuity. I'm sure you can find a way. I don't care how you do it, just get the job done."

"Or what?" I asked.

Luciana smiled again.

She had an ace up her sleeve, and she relished playing it. "I thought I might encounter some resistance from you, so I purchased an insurance plan. You two are going to do as I say and keep your mouth shut. You're not going to report this to the Sheriff's Office, or the FBI, or anyone else. If you do this for me, we can all go about our lives like we never met. But if you refuse, or you go to your friends at the department, or you try to fuck me on this in any way, then things aren't going to turn out so well for your sister."

I clenched my jaw, and my hands balled into fists. My face flushed red. "What have you done with her?"

"Don't worry. She's safe, for now. It's really simple. Just do as I ask, then I'll let her go. If you don't, well... I will make sure she suffers."

"I swear to God, if anything happens to her, I'll kill you!"

Luciana chuckled. "You are in no position to make threats."

Luciana called across the water to the neighboring boat. There were thugs with machine guns at the bow and stern. Another thug emerged from the cockpit with a pistol at Madison's head. His hand gripped her arm. She was gagged and bound at the wrists.

My blood boiled.

Rage filled my veins.

Hate radiated from deep inside me.

Madison's brow knitted together, and her eyes looked sad and terrified. Tears streamed down her cheek.

A diabolical grin curled on Luciana's full lips. "What's it going to be?"

30

I had no choice but to comply with Luciana's demands. I couldn't risk Madison's life.

And I was going to handle this my way.

No cops. No FBI. I couldn't take a chance on this getting screwed up. And there was no telling who Luciana had on the payroll.

I exchanged a glance with JD, and as always, he was on board with whatever I decided. He was always there when I needed him in a pinch.

Luciana and her goons left us on the water. They boarded her yacht and sailed away into the darkness.

"I'm sorry, man," Rick said. "She threatened my wife, and my dogs. My fucking dogs! I couldn't say anything."

As soon as he said dogs, I thought about Buddy.

"What exactly happened to Glenn?" I asked.

"She shot him. She wanted us to dive again without a proper

surface interval. Glenn refused. She put two shots into his chest."

Rick slumped, and his eyes welled with tears. "I screwed up. We just wanted to make a little extra money. Times have been tight, lately. Diego said he could move the product. It was way too big for us to handle."

"What about Carlos?" I asked.

"They put him in a fucking wood chipper. A wood chipper, man. These people are ruthless."

"Why?"

"He was Diego's half-brother. They had orchestrated the hit on her."

"Nice lady," JD quipped. He ribbed me a little. "You sure can pick'em."

"There's no way to bring that coke up on her timeline," Rick said.

I thought about it for moment.

"Am I in trouble?" Rick asked. "I mean, am I going to go to jail?"

"You committed multiple felonies," I said.

His face twisted, and he looked like he was going to cry.

"I'm sure if you cooperate, and assist the department, I could put in a good word," I said.

"What ever you need, man! I want to make this right."

"We could dive in shifts," JD said. "Use a winch to pull up the merchandise. If we devise a good system, it might go faster than anticipated."

"I've got a better idea," I said. "Let's go talk to Ian. Maybe we could use the ROV? The *Explorer 2*."

JD's eyes brightened. "Good thinking!"

He moved into the salon to the main helm and cranked up the engines. The water burbled and foamed near the swim platform. He throttled up and we headed back to Coconut Key.

We dropped Rick off at *Diver Down*.

"Go home," I said. "Sit tight."

"I meant it when I said I wanted to help," Rick asserted.

"If you want to help, go home and get your wife and pets out of town."

He reluctantly agreed and shuffled away down the dock.

My thoughts turned to Buddy.

No one was looking after him.

I raced down the dock, and pushed into *Diver Down*. Alejandro was working behind the bar, about to close up for the evening. There were only a few regulars inside.

"What's going on with Madison?" Alejandro asked.

"When was the last time you talked to her?"

"I got a strange phone call from her a few hours ago. Said something came up and she needed me to look after the bar. She was gone when I got here."

I raced to the stairs and bolted up to her loft above the restaurant. The door was unlocked, which wasn't unusual. I burst into her apartment and scanned the area.

My heart pounded in my chest.

I breathed a sigh of relief when I saw Buddy in his crate. I knelt down and opened the door and Buddy ran into my arms. I held him up, and he licked my face.

I loved on him for a moment. "It's okay, boy. I got you now."

He wagged his tail excitedly, but he was still trembling. It had been hours since Madison had been abducted, and the poor thing was all alone. Fortunately, she put his water bowl and food in the crate.

I needed to find someone to look after him while I took care of business. I didn't know how long I'd be gone.

I emptied the water from his dog bowl in the sink and poured the dog food back into the bag. Then I tossed everything into the crate and carried Buddy in one arm and the supplies in the other.

I descended the stairs, traipsed through the bar, and pushed into the parking lot.

I met JD on the dock.

His face crinkled with confusion. "Who's this?"

"This is Petty Officer First Class Buddy."

Buddy barked, but he calmed down after JD petted him.

"I figured the ship could use a good first mate."

Jack arched a curious eyebrow. "Is he housebroken?"

"Yes," I assured.

"Don't you think you should have checked with your landlord to see if pets were allowed?"

"It's always easier to ask for forgiveness, isn't it?" I smiled.

"Tell my ex-wife that," JD muttered.

"I'm thinking Scarlett could look after him while we go on this adventure," I said.

JD agreed. "I've got her staying with a friend right now. I told her to get out of the house as soon as I found out about Madison. If Luciana is looking to hit us where it hurts, Scarlett's not safe either. I told her to take one of my pistols for good measure."

"Does she know how to use it?"

"Learned from the best," JD boasted.

"I don't remember teaching her," I said.

His scowled at me.

JD and I climbed into the red Porche and drove to Scarlett's friend's apartment. Haley lived at the *Ocean View Estates* which, ironically, didn't have an ocean view.

It was a second floor walk up apartment. #209, building G. A guy answered the door when we knocked. He looked about 20, and had a high-and-tight haircut. Either he liked to keep it short for the summer, or he was a jar head.

The bulldog tattoo he had to on his shoulder suggested the latter. It just peeked out beyond his sleeve and told me that he had spent some time at Parris Island.

"I'm Scarlett's dad," JD said.

"Yes, sir. Come right in, sir. I'm Brian."

He shook hands with JD and me, and introductions were made. He held the door for us as we stepped into the small, but well appointed apartment.

The girls went gaga over Buddy.

I released him from the crate, and Haley and Scarlett instantly dropped to the ground to play with him.

I gave them instructions on his care. "Do you think you can handle him?"

Scarlett flashed me a sassy look. "I can take better care of him than you can."

The girls baby-talked Buddy, and he licked their faces. They were all smiles and giggles, smitten with the little guy.

"He's adorable," Scarlett said. "Where did you get him?"

"We don't have time to be screwing around," JD said.

"What's going on?" Scarlett asked.

"Madison's been taken," I said.

Scarlett's eyes went wide, and her jaw dropped.

"I need you to sit tight," JD said. "Don't leave this apartment. Don't let anybody in. Does everybody understand?"

"Yes sir," Brian said.

JD looked at the new Marine. "You, Devil Dog. I'm expecting you to look after these women."

Brian stood tall, puffing his chest with pride. "Yes, sir!"

"What's your MOS, Marine?" JD asked.

"0311, Rifleman. I'm on 10 day leave before SOI."

I could see that JD felt comforted by the fact an infantry Marine would be looking after the girls.

We left Hailey's apartment, and went to roust Ian out of bed. Hopefully he'd be inclined to assist us.

31

I an didn't live far from the Institute, and had a luxurious Oceanside house. The two-story had a midcentury modern vibe to it. Sweeping lines, graceful curves, lots of glass that blended interior and exterior spaces.

Though the Institute was a nonprofit organization, Ian had amassed a small fortune from his patents prior to funding the Oceanographic Institute.

It was almost midnight when we banged on the door. It took the white-haired man several minutes to answer. When he finally did, he was not too pleased about it. He pulled open the door wearing fuzzy slippers and a robe. "You know what time it is?"

"I need your help," JD said. "It's an emergency."

Ian stepped onto the porch and pulled the door closed behind him. Then he hissed, "Why the hell should I help you? You haven't done anything that I asked you to do."

"Things have gotten rather complicated," JD said. "But I promise, I will run surveillance for you."

A sour look crinkled on Ian's face for a moment, then he finally relented. "What do you need?

"We need to borrow the *Explorer 2*."

His eyes widened with astonishment. "Absolutely not! Do you know how expensive that prototype is?"

"This is an emergency," JD said.

"What the hell are you going to do with it?"

JD and I exchanged a glance.

"Police business," JD said.

Ian's face crinkled. "Police business my ass. Tell me what you're doing with it, or you don't get it."

JD shared the story with him.

"Well why didn't you just say so in the first place?"

JD shrugged.

"Let me get dressed, then we can go to the Institute." He slipped back inside and emerged a few moments later wearing white pants and a white shirt. "Follow me there," he said as he climbed into his Jeep.

Ian cranked up the engine, dropped the vehicle in reverse, and backed out of the driveway. The tires chirped as he dropped it into first gear and sped down the road.

At the Institute, he slid a key card into a slot, then accessed the building and deactivated the alarm with the code. We followed him into the lab where he gave us a brief overview of the *Explorer 2*. "It has a remote onboard battery pack that's good for roughly 8 hours of continuous use. It's still a prototype, so there are a few bugs. And I only have one version of the hardware controller."

He handed us the controller that had multiple joysticks. An attached screen displayed angles from multiple onboard cameras. "This will allow you to control the *Explorer 2*."

I fiddled with the joysticks.

"That's not a toy," Ian cautioned.

I flashed an apologetic glance.

"The articulated arms have pressure sensitive grip pads. They can pick up a lead weight, or a wineglass. It's able to sense the different densities and not shatter delicate objects. All due to the advanced software and hardware that I designed, of course."

"Of course," I muttered.

His eyes narrowed at me, then he cleared his throat. "As I was saying, this is a very expensive prototype. One of a kind. Please be careful with it."

"We will return it without a scratch," JD assured.

We loaded the *Explorer* and the controller into padded transport cases. Ian found an equipment cart and rolled it over to the table. We loaded the gear onto it and pushed our new toy out of the lab and loaded it into JD's Porsche.

"You boys be careful out there," Ian said.

We thanked him and headed back to *Diver Down*.

At the marina, we lugged the equipment down the dock and transferred the gear onto the *Wild Tide* and made ready to get underway.

32

A   t the dive site we set up the control center and launched the ROV.

I grabbed the joysticks and guided it to the murky depths. The *Explorer 2* sank into the inky blackness. I hoped it would be narrow enough to fit through the submersible's hatch, but I wasn't holding my breath.

Despite its size, the *Explorer* was powerful. It was a little challenging to fight against the current, but I kept it on target.

The running lights illuminated the path ahead, and after some searching, I managed to find the submersible.

I sat in the cockpit, looking at the glow of the control screen as I navigated toward the target.

Once I reached the submersible, I hovered over the hatch and used the navigational thrusters to angle the *Explorer* toward the narrow portal. I plunged the craft inside, then weaved through the internal compartments.

I glided the ROV into the cargo area and extended the articulated arm. It took a little doing, but I managed to snag a brick of cocaine, after several failed attempts.

Among the many uses the craft had been designed for, placing limpet mines on the hulls of enemy ships was one of them. The little craft was right at home carrying objects up to 15 pounds. But the large packages, containing multiple kilos, were too heavy for the unit. Those had to be sliced open, and the individual kilos removed.

I spun the vehicle around 180°, retraced my steps through the sub and exited through the hatch and navigated across the seafloor. I released the brick of cocaine into a wire-grid crab net. Once the net was full, we hoisted it up with a motorized winch.

The process was long, arduous, and exacting. It took roughly 10 minutes to grab a brick and drop it in the net.

There were thousands of bricks in the submarine.

At this rate, we'd be here for days.

A sick feeling twisted in my stomach. A mist of sweat coated my skin. "This isn't going to work."

"I'll be eligible for Social Security by the time we finish pulling all of these bricks up," JD said.

We had amassed a small stack on the deck, but it was nothing compared to what was left in the sub—nearly 8 tons of cocaine.

"Why don't we just lift the whole damn thing?" JD suggested. "Gotta be easier than this. A couple lift bags and presto."

"I think it's a little more complicated than that."

"I know a guy who might be able to help."

"My friend, Kurt, runs a salvage operation. He pulls boats out of the water all the time. I know he can handle this," JD assured.

We'd been at it most of the night and didn't have much to show for our efforts.

By the time we recovered the ROV, the morning sun was cresting over the water. The orange ball of flame glimmered across the waves. I was tired, distraught, and time was running out.

I had one more sunrise to figure this out.

JD called Kurt, and an hour later we met him at the harbor that was home to his salvage operation.

Kurt was mid 30s, curly brown hair, blue eyes, and an athletic build. His tanned skin had seen plenty of hours in the sun.

He had an offshore support tug with a red hull and a white bridge. It was 40 meters long, had a draft of 4 meters, and 2 CAT diesel engines putting out close to 8000 hp. The tug had a top speed of 15 knots and a bollard pull of 80 tons. It had a forward towing winch, a deck crane, and a single drum towing winch.

There were 10 spacious cabins, a large wheelhouse, a ship's office, multiple storage compartments, and even a small gym. It was equipped with radar, satellite data systems, echo-sounder, sat telephone, gyro stabilizer, auxiliary generators, and more. It was capable of multiple salvage and support operations, including fire-fighting.

"Now, what is it you're trying to bring up again?" Kurt asked.

JD and I exchanged a glance, then he pulled out his badge. "I don't know if I mentioned it, but we're working with the Sheriff's Department now. What I'm about to tell you is official police business, and must be kept confidential."

"Sure thing."

"We're trying to recover a narco sub in 110 feet of water."

"What size is it?"

"75 feet. Fiberglass and Kevlar hull, with reinforced steel beams." I said.

"How much cargo?"

"Roughly 8 tons, give or take."

"No problem. We do this all the time for the Coast Guard and the DEA. I've pulled Go-Fast boats out of the water, planes, submersibles, you name it. Why don't you just call the DEA? Isn't this their turf, anyway?"

"This is a very sensitive operation," JD said. "We are deep undercover right now and we have concerns that someone in the agency may be leaking information."

It was total bullshit.

Kurt's eyes widened. "Really?"

JD nodded.

"I can salvage it for you. Am I billing the county for this?"

JD and I exchanged another glance.

"How much is this going to cost?" JD asked.

"If I'm billing the county... $25,000."

Both of our eyes widened.

"What?" JD exclaimed.

"If you don't think that's reasonable, you can find somebody else to do it. The going rate is $150 to $250 a foot for harbor salvage. This is the open ocean. Factor in depth and hazards. I've got my lift bags, my crew, fuel, plus my time, and the added risk... $335 a foot is a reasonable fee."

"What if we are not billing the county on this one?" JD asked.

Kurt's eyes narrowed at him. His suspicious gaze flicked between the two of us. "What are you up to?"

"Like I said. This is very undercover, top-secret type stuff. National security," JD said.

Kurt rolled his eyes. He definitely smelled something fishy. "You two aren't thinking about salvaging the cargo and hustling it on your own, are you?"

"How long have you known me?" JD asked. "Would I do something like that?"

"Yes," Kurt said flatly, without hesitation.

Jack feigned offense. "I'm hurt that you would think of me in such a way."

"Cut the shit, JD. I'm not helping you do something illegal."

"It's not technically illegal," JD said.

"The cartel is holding my sister hostage," I said. "If I don't get the cargo up, she's going to die."

That changed Kurt's stance. "Why don't you go to the feds?"

I shook my head. "No way. They'll kill her. And trust me, anyone operating at this level has sources in high places. I'm not taking a chance that they've got a mole in the bureau. These kinds of people pay off cops all the time."

Kurt grimaced and let out a deep breath. "I'm not gonna get in trouble for doing this, am I?"

"We are the police," JD assured. "Nobody's going to get in trouble for anything."

Kurt hesitated for a long moment. He didn't look like he was going to agree to our cockamamy scheme.

33

"**O**kay. Fuel, equipment, and crew... I can do it for $7000. That's a friend price."

"$5000," JD countered.

"$6500. Take it or leave it."

"Deal," I said before JD had a chance to protest.

"We need to get a move on," JD said.

"I can't do it today," Kurt said. "I've got clients."

We both looked at him, incredulous.

"What part of *life and death* did you not understand?" JD said. "This needs to happen yesterday."

"I can't cancel my client."

"Tell them this is urgent police business. Lives are at stake," JD growled.

After a moment, Kurt relented. "Okay. Fine. I'll see what I can do."

Kurt made some calls and cleared his schedule. As far as his crew knew, this was just an average day on the water assisting local law enforcement.

We boarded the *Wild Tide*, and Kurt followed us in the tug back to the dive site.

It was midmorning, and the sun was already high in the sky. We were out on the open water in broad daylight, trying to raise a drug sub. It was so blatantly obvious that we had some type of heavy operation going that I hoped no one would pay us any attention.

We took a tender over to the tug, tied it off, and boarded.

Kurt sent two of his divers into the water with marine lift bags. They were state-of-the-art yellow salvage bags with pressure release valves and attached tanks of compressed air. The divers attached two bags to cleats on the bow, and two bags on the stern. Then the divers would open the valves on the tanks and inflate the lift bags when everything was rigged.

Fully inflated, they looked like giant yellow propane tanks. Each one was capable of hoisting 6000 tons. Four of them could easily lift the submersible. The pressure release valves would automatically let air escape during ascent.

The first set of divers attached the bags. The second set filled them with oxygen. Within 45 minutes of our arrival, Kurt's crew had the submersible floating at the surface of the ocean.

I couldn't believe my eyes.

My jaw dropped, and I exchanged an ecstatic glance with JD.

"You were seriously going to charge $25,000 to do that?" JD asked. "It took you 45 minutes?"

"That's why I charge $25,000. These other ass-clowns might be out here for a day or two and still not get it up."

I couldn't disagree with him. He was worth every penny.

The divers attached a tow line from the tug to the sub.

"What the hell are you going to do with this thing?" Kurt asked.

JD and I consulted.

"What if we tow it to Shrimp Key Island," JD said. "We can beach the sub in the shallows and unload the cargo. Nobody ever goes out there."

"You're talking about a submarine," I said. "It's going to draw a little attention."

"We could just rig it with a bunch of C4 and turn it over to Luciana as is. Let her deal with it." JD smiled.

"Somehow I don't think she's going to like that." I paused. "We have to leverage the exchange. She has no incentive to let any of us live."

"I didn't want to say that, but..."

"Guys." Kurt said. "I don't think you have to worry about that anymore." He pointed to a Coast Guard Defender Class boat on the horizon that was heading our way.

I grimaced, and nerves twisted my stomach.

"If anyone asks, I was acting at the behest of law enforcement," Kurt said. "This shit's all on you."

"No worries," JD said. "I've got this."

JD and I had our badges ready as the Defender pulled alongside.

Several Coast Guard officers stood on the deck with assault rifles. The Chief Petty Officer shouted to us through a bullhorn, "Afternoon, gentlemen. Prepare to be boarded."

Within moments, the aft deck swarmed with officers.

"Tyson Wild, Coconut County Sheriff's Department."

"Chief Petty Officer Duane Richardson. What have you got here?"

"Narco sub. We stumbled across it and thought it would be a good idea to take it into custody."

"Why didn't you call us or the DEA? This is a little out of your territory, isn't it?"

"It's complicated," I said. "We are working a murder investigation. We followed the suspects to this location, then ascertained that they were trying to recover the drugs from the sub. We acted quickly to confiscate the contraband before it disappeared. Frankly, I didn't want to take the chance of missing the opportunity. I understand that we probably didn't follow protocol in the situation, but it seemed justifiable."

"Well, next time, just make sure you call someone in the Joint Task Force, the FBI, the Coast Guard, or the DEA. It's a federal matter."

"You're totally right," I said.

"No harm, no foul," Richardson said. "Why don't you tow this thing to the task force headquarters in Key West?"

"Whoa, hang on a minute there," JD said. "We want credit for this bust!"

"Trust me, you'll get credit."

"No way," JD protested. "There's 8 tons of cocaine in that sub. I want my picture in the paper as we bring this thing into the harbor. I can see the headline now... *Coconut Key Sheriffs make largest drug bust in Florida's history!*"

Richardson rolled his eyes. "This isn't the largest drug bust in Florida history."

"Well, maybe we can fudge a little bit," JD said.

Richardson took a deep breath, clearly getting annoyed with the two of us.

I crossed my fingers hoping this would go our way.

34

"Let me contact my commander and see how he wants to handle this," Richardson said.

JD and I waited with bated breath while Richardson radioed in. There were a few minutes of back-and-forth, then he turned to us with a grim look. "No dice. Commander says it's gotta go with us."

My whole body tensed, and my throat tightened. I exchanged a nervous glance with JD.

We continued to protest, but it didn't do any good.

JD leaned toward Kurt and muttered in his ear, "Looks like you're billing the Coast Guard for this one."

Kurt didn't mind. It meant he'd get his full rate.

Kurt's crew pumped out the water from the submersible, and the Coast Guard confiscated the entire load. They transferred 8 tons of cocaine onto the patrol boat, then scuttled the sub we had worked so hard to raise.

Richardson had us fill out paperwork while the operation was underway. Once everything was completed, the Coast Guard went on their way.

Richardson assured us we would get full credit for the bust.

I couldn't care less. My only chance of saving Madison had vanished.

JD and I thanked Kurt for the effort and took the tender back to the *Wild Tide*. There were still 50kg of cocaine aboard that we had retrieved the previous night.

I was inconsolable.

My body slumped, and my face was grim. I didn't say a word.

"We'll figure this thing out," JD said, trying to assure me.

"Madison could be anywhere."

"They're keeping her on the yacht. That much is certain," JD said.

"Isabella is unable to track Luciana's phone. She probably ditched it."

"If I were her, I would change phones every few days." He thought for a moment. "I'm sure they took Madison's phone too. They probably tossed it overboard."

"Luciana's a smart woman. She wouldn't have gotten this far if she wasn't."

It was afternoon. I was hungry, tired, and dehydrated. My skin crackled from the sun burn. I had forgotten to put sunscreen on with all the commotion. My head throbbed, and my anxiousness caused my stomach to twist and rumble with acid.

"If it's any consolation, the plan wouldn't have worked anyway," JD said. "The minute she had that cocaine, she would have killed us all. You know that?"

"I would have liked to think we'd have found a way to avoid that."

We were silent for a long moment. The boat rocked back and forth on the waves.

I had no game plan.

No next move.

The only thing I could do was wait for Luciana's call, tell her we had the cargo, and buy a little time.

JD moved into the salon and started the engines.

I sat in the cockpit, moping.

The boat rumbled as he throttled up and headed back toward Coconut Key.

We arrived at the marina at *Diver Down* in less than an hour. The sun had dipped below the horizon and the sky was lavender. Sea birds squawked and circled the marina in a flurry before the roost. I gazed at the restaurant as we idled past the rows of boats. It seemed so empty, knowing Madison wasn't there.

I was so mad at myself. This was all my fault. I kept thinking I should never have come back to Coconut Key. I was just putting the people I cared about in jeopardy.

I let myself wallow in my own misery for a few more

moments, then I decided this was counterproductive. I was focusing on the wrong thing. I was thinking about everything that had gone wrong, and how horrible the situation was instead of focusing on solutions.

There is always a way.

Nothing is impossible.

My phone buzzed in my pocket. It was from an unknown caller. "Hello?"

Luciana's angry voice filtered through the speaker. "Please tell me the cocaine that the Coast Guard just confiscated from a submersible isn't mine?"

I hesitated, and a slight grin curled on my lips. She had called me from a burner phone. I was sure Isabella could now find her position. And it would be recent.

"What?" I asked, playing dumb.

"I have a source that told me a salvage crew raised a submersible and the Coast Guard seized nearly 8 tons of cocaine. I don't know about you, but that scenario sounds awfully familiar."

"You know how many drug subs there are out there?" I said. "It's pure coincidence."

"Really? My source tells me this cocaine was stamped with my logo. You want to explain that to me?"

"Okay. You got me. We ran into a little trouble."

"A little trouble?" she said, incensed.

"I'm going to get it back," I assured.

"You're going to steal the cocaine from the Coast Guard?"

"Well, actually, it will be transferred to the DEA. They'll handle it from there."

"I've decided I'm not going to kill your sister. Not right away. I'm going to torture her and make her death as miserable as possible, dragging it out for as long as I can."

"I have connections," I said. "I can get it back."

"I don't believe you."

"If anything happens to Madison, you are never getting your cargo. Give me another day. I will figure something out."

She huffed. The line was silent for a long moment. "I know I don't have to explain this to you, but I am not the only person you are dealing with here. There are people I work for that are very displeased. They lack my patience—and I am a saint in comparison."

"One more day."

"Fine. But if I don't get what I want, I'm coming for you and everyone you know. Have I made myself clear?"

"Crystal."

She hung up, and I immediately dialed Isabella.

"I need you to track the last number that called this phone," I said.

"I'll see what I can do," Isabella said, then she hung up.

35

We had no sooner docked the boat when Isabella called me back with Luciana's cell phone coordinates. JD and I looked it up on the map.

"That's Coral Key," JD announced.

"There's nothing out there. It's just an empty island."

"Maybe it's not so empty anymore," I said.

JD moved to the helm, and I cast off the lines. We idled out of the marina, then throttled up, and headed toward Coral Key.

We needed to get there as soon as possible. I didn't have up-to-the-minute tracking information, and I wanted to get there before Luciana moved again.

The engines rumbled as we raced across the ocean, carving through the waves. The sky grew dark and the moon rose over the water.

I felt like I had guzzled a pot of coffee, adrenaline coursing through my veins.

JD cut the running lights and slowed the boat about a mile away from Coral Key. We moved forward at about 5 knots. I dashed to the bow and scanned the horizon with night vision goggles. The green optics illuminated the island as plain as day.

JD cut the engines, and we drifted on the water.

Luciana had built a luxury home on the island. A long dock went from the house to the water where the yacht was docked.

It was an island oasis.

A luxury escape for those who could afford such a place.

It was remote enough that she could do just about anything she wanted here.

"You think Madison is there?" JD asked.

"We're about to find out," I said. "Get the drone."

JD moved into the salon and returned a moment later with a Pelican case that housed the drone and its controller. He unlatched the case, and we took the prototype out of the custom cut padding.

I took out the controller. It had two joysticks and several auxiliary knobs and buttons along with an attached screen —similar in design to the *Explorer 2's* controller.

JD closed the case, and we set the drone on top of it. It would provide a stable platform to launch the device from.

We powered the craft on, and it went through a series of diagnostic checks before giving a green light.

The drone had built-in stabilizers and GPS navigation. Through a companion cell phone app, you could create flight plans, or choose from pre-programmed routes.

I turned on the propulsion system, and the tiny blades spun. After I familiarized myself with the controls, I lifted the craft into the air.

It pitched and rolled as I learned to steady it. I buzzed it around the deck for a moment. Once I felt comfortable, I sent it racing across the water toward the yacht.

The drone was 6x6 and virtually silent. It was painted in a dull matte black color that made it difficult to see at night. Ian had gone to great lengths to make sure this was a military grade product, perfect for stealth reconnaissance operations. Equipped with night vision, infrared, and an onboard 8K camera, it was our best chance of finding Madison.

I circled the drone around Luciana's yacht. With the infrared vision, warm bodies showed up as an orange-red color, while cooler areas of the frame were blue. I counted three people on board. They were all above deck and carrying assault rifles.

That ruled out Madison's presence.

I followed the dock toward the house and buzzed the drone overhead.

The house had two stories, raised on concrete stilts. Wood decking circled the house, and the back deck had a jacuzzi. A staircase descended to the forest of mangrove trees, and a narrow path led to the beach.

I saw four orange blobs around the house. One moved around inside. Another circled the property outside, walking around the deck. There was an orange body in what appeared to be a second-story bedroom, and another body in a separate second-floor bedroom.

I hovered the drone outside the window and moved toward the glass. Through the blinds I was able to see Luciana lying in bed, watching TV.

I backed the drone away from the window and circled around to the other bedroom. Inside, I saw Madison— bound at the wrists and ankles with duct tape across her mouth.

My blood boiled, seeing her like that.

My heart pumped with excitement and the possibility of a rescue.

I increased the altitude on the drone and circled the house again watching the movement pattern of the outside guard.

He was armed with an assault rifle.

I pulled back and took a broader view of the island and circled the area.

The whole island wasn't much longer than a few football fields, and almost as wide.

I set the drone on autopilot to return to its point of origin, and within a few minutes, the drone hovered over the deck. Since we had drifted slightly, I adjusted its position and landed it manually on the deck.

"What's the plan?" JD asked.

"I'm going to take the tender around to the east side of the island. I need you to create a distraction."

JD smiled. "I love creating distractions."

"Take the *Explorer 2* and put a limpet mine on the hull of the *Liquid Asset*. When I give you the signal, blow it. With any luck, the guards in the house will rush to see what's happened. I'll get Madison and escape via the tender. Then I'll meet you back here."

"Once I detonate the mine, I'll move the boat around to the east side and provide overwatch," JD said.

"How effective are your sniper skills from a moving platform?" I asked.

"I used to drop enemy targets from the door of a helicopter. This wouldn't be much different. Just gotta role with the tide."

I gave him a skeptical glance. It had been a long time since he did anything like that. I'd be surprised if he'd be able to hit the broad side of a barn now.

36

I prepped my gear, and we launched the tender. It was the same 7.5 foot inflatable *WavePro MK-II* from the *Slick'n Salty*. The pontoons were gray and black, and it had a *Barracuda MM7* electric motor that would run at close to 6 knots.

The motor was whisper quiet.

I climbed into the tender and cast-off. I twisted the throttle, and the electric barracuda motor buzzed away from the *Wild Tide*.

I bounced against the waves and banked around to the east side of the island. I was decked out in full tactical gear— helmet, night vision goggles, tactical headset, tactical vest, 9mm pistol, assault rifle, extra magazines, smoke canisters, fragmentation grenades, C4 explosive and detonators.

I liked to be prepared.

Once I reached the desolate side of the island, I cut the engine and glided in on the surf. I hopped out of the tender in the shallows and pulled it onto the sandy beach, dragging it up to the tree line where I hid it in the underbrush.

The area was thick with mangroves, shrubs, and tall grass.

I tapped my headset. "The Eagle has landed. I'll contact you when I'm in position."

"Copy that," JD said, his voice crackling in my ear.

The dappled rays of moonlight cascaded through the mangrove trees. I advanced through the underbrush with my weapon in the firing position, weaving through the trees, soundless.

I held up at the tree line near the house, taking cover behind a tree and some shrubs. I looked through a thermal imaging scope and scanned the property, looking for the guards. I saw one inside, standing in the kitchen, making a sandwich. Luciana was still in bed watching TV, and I assumed Madison was still in the spare bedroom.

I watched as the other guard circled the house.

He stopped in the back and lit a cigarette. The cherry glowed red as he inhaled a deep breath. Then he blew a thick cloud into the air. It drifted away and dissipated into the trees.

"We are a go on *Operation Titanic*," I whispered. "I repeat, we are a go on *Operation Titanic*."

"Copy that!"

A moment later the dull thump of the limpet mine rumbled through the air.

I could feel the vibration through the souls my feet, even at this distance.

Water splashed in the air, and the panicked voices of the people on board the *Liquid Asset* echoed across the island.

The guard in the back yard dropped his cigarette and stamped it out.

Just as I'd hoped, he ran around to the front of the house and sprinted down the dock. So did the guard who was making a sandwich in the kitchen.

I watched the thermal image of Luciana leap out of bed and sprint down the stairs to the front of the house. She disappeared through the front doorway.

I slipped the thermal scope into a pocket and climbed the stairs. I advanced across the deck and pushed into the house through a sliding glass door that was unlocked.

The house was well decorated and had an elegant, but beachy vibe. It was like a luxury tropical resort.

I spiraled up the staircase, advanced down the hall, and kicked open the spare bedroom door.

Madison's eyes widened with relief.

She mumbled something but I couldn't make out what she said through the duct tape.

I slung my rifle, drew my tactical knife, and advanced to the bed. The sharp black blade cut the ropes around her wrists and ankles. I peeled the tape from her mouth, then put my finger to my lips, indicating she shouldn't say a word.

I handed her my pistol. "Follow me."

I pushed into the hallway and crept toward the stairs. A quick scan of the living room below revealed it was empty.

With the wave of my hand, I motioned Madison forward, and we descended the steps and slipped out the sliding glass door.

Everything was going according to plan.

We raced across the deck, plowed down the staircase, and weaved through the underbrush. Within a few paces, we were at the tree line by the beach.

I grabbed the tender and hauled it toward the surf.

That's when things got complicated.

The snap of bullets cracked the air.

They zipped past me, and I felt the breeze on my skin.

I ducked for cover and dashed back to the tree line.

The bullets punctured the inflatable pontoons of the tender, and air whistled as it rushed out of the holes.

Within moments, the craft deflated.

We weren't going to be making a quick escape.

I angled my weapon around the trunk of a tree and blasted several shots in the direction of the gun fire. Muzzle flash flickered, and the smell of gunpowder wafted to my nose as my assault rifle hammered against my shoulder.

Another flurry of shots peppered the surrounding trees, splintering shards of wood and disturbing leaves.

I told Madison to stay down.

She hugged the dirt.

I scanned the tree line with my NOD (Night Optical Device), looking for the thug. I caught a glimpse of him hiding behind a mangrove tree. As he angled his weapon around the trunk, I blasted several rounds. The bullets punctured his throat, and the force of impact sent him crashing down. His weapon fell to the sand, and he twitched on the ground for a few moments.

Footsteps in the underbrush drew my attention.

I spun toward the house to see another guard advancing toward us. Before I could get my weapon aimed, Madison blasted two shots with the hand cannon.

She double tapped the goon in the chest, and dark blood spurted out, glimmering in the moonlight. He fell back into the grass, and blood gurgled as his chest sucked air into the wound.

I was impressed.

My father had taught her how to shoot at a young age, but I didn't know if she had kept up with it.

Apparently she still had skills.

There were at least three more cartel soldiers on the island, plus Luciana.

I didn't want to stay in one position for too long.

We advanced southbound along the tree line, then took a position slightly inland, about 30 yards away.

I scanned the area with my night vision goggles. A moment later three more goons marched through the underbrush, walking abreast. They had their rifles shouldered and scanned the darkness.

But they didn't have night vision.

I took aim at the nearest one, pointing my IR laser at his chest. The beam, only visible with a NOD, slashed the night. My finger squeezed the trigger, snapping off two rounds. An instant later, his chest exploded.

He crashed through the leaves, and the two others spun in my direction and opened fire.

Once again, a flurry of bullets peppered the trees around me.

I lined up another goon with my IR laser and squeezed off a quick burst of fire, then aimed at the last goon.

It was like shooting paper targets.

The thugs fell to the ground amid a flurry of bullets.

The forest was suddenly quiet again.

The crickets resumed chirping.

I looked to Madison. "Are you okay?"

She nodded, still hugging the dirt.

I tapped my headset. "Overwatch, do you copy?"

"Sounds like you're making friends," JD said.

"People love me, what can I say?"

"Need a hand?"

"I think I've got this one under control," I said. "But there's a slight problem with the tender."

"What do you mean?"

"It doesn't exist anymore," I said. "We're at the southeast corner of the island. How close do you think you can get to shore?"

"I've got a pretty shallow draft on the boat. Maybe 50 yards?"

I looked to Madison. "You feel comfortable swimming through the surf?"

Madison nodded. "No sweat. I've still got some of my swim team chops."

I tapped my headset. "Pull around and look for my signal."

"Copy that."

A few minutes later, I saw the *Wild Tide* pull close to shore. I flashed my tactical light twice, and JD hovered the boat in position.

I moved to the tree line and surveyed the beach. It looked clear. "Go!"

"What about you?" Madison asked.

"I'm right behind you. I need to take care of a few things."

She hesitated.

"Go!"

Madison ran across the beach and splashed into the surf. She dove in and started swimming toward the *Wild Tide*.

I watched for a few moments, then spun around and headed

toward the house. Luciana had caused this mess, and I was going to see to it that she did time in prison.

There was an eerie stillness on the island. The air was thick and humid, and the crickets continued to chirp in a pulsating rhythm.

I crept through the mangrove trees, moving through the tall grass. The bodies of the fallen guards lay near the stairs to the back deck. I stepped over them, moved to the steps, and sneaked up the stairs.

With my infrared scope, I scanned the house.

I didn't see Luciana's heat signature anywhere.

I put the IR scope back in my vest and lowered my NODs witch were affixed to my tactical helmet. I pushed across the deck and into the house.

I crept through the living room sweeping my rifle across the space. I cleared the downstairs, then the upstairs, then exited the front of the house.

My head swiveled from side to side as I scanned the west side of the island and advanced down the dock.

The *Liquid Asset* had taken on a considerable amount of water. But in the shallows surrounding the island, it didn't have far to sink.

In the distance, I heard the whine of an outboard motor, and I caught sight of Luciana attempting to escape in a tender. The tiny craft plowed against the surf as she headed out to sea.

I tapped my headset again. "Overwatch, pick me up on the west side dock. We've got a runner!"

37

J D navigated to the dock, and I climbed on board. He reversed away from the peer, then angled the boat around and chased after Luciana in the tender.

She had a considerable head start, but at 6 to 7 knots an hour, she couldn't outrun us.

The *Wild Tide* sliced through the water, approaching the small inflatable. I saw muzzle flash illuminate the darkness and heard a bang!

The front windshield pitted and webbed with cracks as a bullet struck it.

JD ducked and veered the boat away. "That bitch just shot at us!"

"What did you expect?" I mumbled.

JD growled, and his face twisted.

Luciana fired several more shots, pelting the boat. The impacts thumped and pinged against the hull.

"God dammit!" JD growled again. "This boat is brand-new." He scowled at me, perturbed. "Would you get out there and shoot her?"

"We're taking her in. She's going down for this," I said.

JD circled around the tender, and Luciana continued to shoot at the boat. A wake of white water tossed the tiny inflatable around.

JD made another pass, buzzing close by the tender, and Luciana fired two more shots at the boat.

When we circled back around, I saw that the wake had capsized the tender.

I sprinted to the cockpit and leaned over the gunwale, searching the water with my night vision.

The capsized tender rose and fell on the waves, but I didn't see any sign of Luciana.

JD stopped the boat and idled around the inflatable.

The engines burbled and the smell of exhaust wafted through the air.

The night was still.

Nobody was shooting at us anymore.

Madison stepped into the cockpit, but I told her to get back into the salon and stay down. I didn't want to take any chances.

Using the bow and stern thrusters, JD navigated close to the tender. I grabbed it with a hook and pulled it to the gunwale and flipped it over.

It was empty.

There was no sign of Luciana in the water.

JD turned on the underwater lights, and we searched the area for another 30 minutes before giving up.

"I think she drowned," JD said.

"I don't know. That woman is evil. And evil is hard to kill."

"Maybe the sharks will get her?" JD said with a grin.

Jack walked around the boat, surveying the damage. He frowned and shook his head, then he moved to the helm, throttled up, and circled back to Coral Key. It was part of Coconut County and within our jurisdiction.

We tied off at the dock, and I scaled the gunwale. "Stay with Madison. I'm going to take a look around."

"Do you think she swam back to shore?" JD asked.

I shrugged. "I don't know. Anything is possible."

I circled the island and marched through the underbrush with my night vision goggles.

The only thing alive on the island were the bugs.

I moved into the house, and searched room by room. I found a large closet full of bricks of cocaine, all stamped with the *Los Demonios* logo.

By the time I returned to the dock, JD had unloaded all the cocaine we had pulled from the narco sub onto the pier. "It's hers anyway, it's not like we're planting evidence," JD said.

I told him I had found additional contraband in the house.

We called Sheriff Daniels, and within an hour, he arrived with the medical examiner and forensics team.

"What the hell is going on here?" Daniels said, eyeing the semi-submerged yacht.

"Luciana kidnapped Madison. I had reason to believe she was in imminent danger. I entered into the home and rescued my sister. As we attempted to make our escape, shots were fired." I kept it by the book.

"Let me guess, everyone's dead? "

"Only the bad people," I said.

The sheriff's stern eyes narrowed at me.

"Luciana was a high-level operative in one of the major cartels," I explained.

Daniels grimaced. "The mayor is going to love this. It's going to be amusing watching him distance himself from her." He paused. "What's the body count?"

"Five. Possibly six," I said. "

His brow crinkled.

"Luciana attempted to escape in a tender. But her boat capsized, and we are assuming she drowned."

The sheriff sighed. "Anything else I need to know?"

I told him Luciana was responsible for Glenn Parker's death.

"Good job," Daniels said with a stone face.

It was rare praise from the stoic man, and it caught me off guard. I let a thin smile tug at my lips.

It took a few hours to wrap things up on the island, document the events, and remove the bodies.

We headed back to Coconut Key, and JD brought the boat on plane. I took a seat on the settee and processed everything that had happened.

The marina at Diver Down was quiet when we arrived—it was the middle of the night. We tied up the boat and reconnected the shore power and water.

JD grabbed a few beers from the galley, and we sat in the cockpit, decompressing.

"I guess I should say thank you," Madison said.

"Just being a protective older brother."

She smiled. "Maybe sometimes that's not so bad."

We almost shared a nice sibling moment, then her face soured.

"But I wouldn't have been in this mess in the first place if it weren't for you!"

"I'm sorry."

"You can't just say you're sorry and think that makes it all better."

"I don't think it makes it all better. But what do you want me to do?"

She was silent for a moment. "So, I'm just supposed to go about my life like this never happened?"

"No. I think you should dwell on it and let it scar you for life," I said with a healthy dose of sarcasm.

She didn't take that too well.

The scowl on her face deepened. "You know, ever since you came back, things have been crazy around here."

"Maybe I should leave?"

"Maybe you should!"

We shared an intense gaze, then she huffed and scaled the transom. She stomped down the dock, her bare feet slapping against the wood.

Mr. Miller poked his head out of his cabin and grumbled. "Would you people keep it down? Decent people are trying to sleep!"

I smiled and waved. "Sorry about that."

He cursed at me under his breath and disappeared back into his cabin.

I exchanged a grim glance with JD.

"I'm sure she'll get over it," JD said.

"Don't count on it."

He looked at his watch, took a last gulp of beer, and crinkled the can. The crackling aluminum sounded like a freight train colliding with a car in the still night air.

I was sure Mr. Miller would yell at us again.

Jack moved into the salon and tossed it in the garbage, then stepped back into the cockpit. "I'm going to hit the hay. I'll drop Buddy by after I pick up Scarlett in the morning."

"Thanks," I said. "Are you sure you don't mind him living on board?"

"Every ship needs a first mate," JD said with a grin.

I watched him stroll down the dock, then I pushed into the salon and descended the staircase to the master stateroom. I was too amped up to get a good night's sleep. I tossed and turned mostly.

The next morning, JD dropped off Buddy. He grabbed the prototypes we had borrowed from Ian and ran them back to the Institute. He said he'd touch base with me later.

I let Buddy out of his crate and loved on him. The little guy licked my face and seemed excited to see me. I let him run around the salon and get comfortable in the space again. Then I attached his leash and took him for a walk.

Afterword, I stopped in *Diver Down* to get something to eat. It took Madison a few moments to stroll over and acknowledge me. She looked tired and frazzled, and I don't think she slept much either.

As she began to speak, I mentally prepared myself to get another tongue lashing.

"Listen, I'm sorry I lashed out at you last night. I was in an... emotional state. I'm sure you can understand. I'm not used to this kind of thing like you are."

"I don't think you ever get used to being kidnapped and threatened."

She paused. In a sincere tone, she said, "Thank you for rescuing me."

"You don't need to thank me. You're family. I'd do anything for you. I—"

She held up her hand, cutting me off. "Nope. Let's just leave it at that. It's too early for serious discussions. What are you having?"

I looked at my watch. It was 11:30 AM. "Shrimp tacos."

"Anything to drink?"

"Diet Coke."

"Coming right up." A thin smile formed on her weary face.

A breaking news update flashed on the TV. A news anchor in an urgent tone said, "Prominent real estate developer Luciana Varga was found dead today in the waters off Coconut Key. A local fisherman recovered the body. Authorities have yet to release any other details. A spokesperson for the development company said that all future plans for the Vista Del Mar area are now on indefinite hold. More on that story tonight at six."

I glanced over to Harlan who was working on a beer. "Looks like you're going to be able to stay in your home."

He frowned at me. "Ah, it's a shithole, anyway. I'm thinking about selling and moving onto a sailboat."

I chuckled. Harlan would find something to grumble about no matter what the situation.

My phone rang as I waited for lunch. It was from a number I didn't recognize.

"Hello?"

"This is Special Agent Peter Cullen with the FBI. I'm trying to get in touch with Deputy Wild."

"This is he."

"I was calling about a ballistic search that you ran on a 9mm slug. It matched a slug involved in one of our unsolved cold cases. I thought maybe we could share information?"

"That sounds great. What have you got?" I asked.

I was hopeful this would provide one more clue to help solve my parents' murders.

Ready for more?

Join my newsletter and find out what happens next.

AUTHOR'S NOTE

Thanks for all the great reviews!

Tyson and JD have more adventures on the way!

If you liked this book, let me know with a review on Amazon.

My Max Mars series is sci-fi with mystery and thriller elements, you might want to check it out.

Thanks for reading!

—*Tripp*

MAX MARS

CONNECT WITH ME

I'm just a geek who loves to write. Follow me on Facebook.

www.trippellis.com

Made in the USA
Columbia, SC
17 November 2019